THE CONJURING
COMEDIENNE

THE MORELVILLE COZIES–BOOK 3

ANNE HAGAN

JUG RUN PRESS LLC

Anne Hagan

To Ellen

PUBLISHED BY:
Jug Run Press, USA
Copyright © 2022

https://annehaganauthor.com/

This is a work of fiction. Names, characters, places and incidents are products of the author's imagination or are actual places used entirely fictitiously and are not to be construed as real. Any resemblance to actual events, organizations, or persons, living or deceased, is entirely coincidental.

❀ Created with Vellum

CHAPTER 1–HATTIE'S HERBS

Hattie's Herbs & Oils
Morelville, Ohio
Monday, September 19th

Hattie waved a hand toward the jars she'd finished filling and labeling. They reordered themselves alphabetically and slid back on the counter to the wall, leaving the workspace in front of her clear. She looked around for her towel and spotted it on an adjacent counter near her sleeping spotted cat. She nodded at the rag and caught it when it flew to her. The Egyptian mau she'd gained when an old roommate couldn't take it on location for a movie shoot with her stretched her paws out, but she didn't open her eyes.

Hattie wiped her hands to remove the dirt from the roots she'd been working with. She heard the rumble of a truck outside and got excited. *My sign is here!* She rushed through the shop that was taking shape and opened the front door to greet the driver.

He was gruff and all business when he stepped inside. "I've got your sign," he said as he glanced around at the walls of shelves, most of them still empty. "It's in a crate. Might fit through the door. It's long but not wide."

"It's going outside, up on the wall, over the door."

"Lady," he said as he took off his ball cap and pushed a hand through his tousled hair, "I don't put them up. I just deliver them. When is the installer scheduled? Today?"

She shrugged. "I'll have to check with the company." She sighed. "You might as well bring it in, then."

He turned and headed outside, toward the back of his truck.

"Will you need help?" she called after him as she followed him.

"No, at least not till I get it down on the lift. Maybe getting it through the door."

She was curious to see the finished sign. He'd said it was in a crate, so she stood just outside the door, holding her anticipation in check. She listened as he shifted things around in the back of the trailer. When she heard him moving forward in the trailer, she couldn't help herself any longer. She left the confines of the doorway and moved toward the rear of the truck.

As she looked up at the approaching crate, she felt a presence come into the space behind her. Half turning her head to look over her shoulder, she saw a man coming toward them. He was still several yards off, but his red aura preceded him. Though he was smiling and appeared harmless, the hair on her arms and on the back of her neck stood up.

Hattie controlled a shiver and thought about returning to the safety of her shop, but before she could move, the driver caught her attention again when he pushed the dolly onto the lift gate and stepped on himself.

The man approaching them spoke. "Need a hand, here?" He pulled up beside Hattie and looked up as the driver punched a button to lower the gate. When it moved, the two of them on the ground stepped backward.

She tried to steal a glance at the older stranger, but she found him looking right at her.

He smiled at her and stuck out a hand. "Elias Penny."

"Hattie Novak," she responded, as she took his hand and shook it briefly. It was warm and uncallused. The strange red aura she'd seen and felt turned white and then receded when they touched.

"Really? You look so familiar, but your name doesn't ring a bell. Did you grow up around here, by chance? Move away, and now you're back?"

"No to all of that," she laughed, now at ease with his inquisitiveness.

"Novak, huh? Any relation to Bridget?"

"She's my aunt; my great aunt."

Elias nodded. "I'd like to say I can see the family resemblance, but that's not it."

"Not what?"

"Why you look familiar. Can't quite place it…"

The lift gate clanged as it touched the ground. The driver pushed the dolly holding the crated sign off and then stepped off behind it. He wheeled the dolly closer to the door then pulled it out from under the crate.

"Just leaving it right there?" Elias asked him.

The driver tipped his head toward Hattie. "She said, inside."

"Here, let me give you a hand then," Elias said. He stepped around Hattie and took up a position on one side of the crate while the driver tipped it back toward himself. The delivery man held his end, waist high, with ease.

"It's not heavy? It should be solid wood." Hattie asked.

Elias Penny squatted and picked up the other end from the ground with a slight grunt. He glanced at Hattie. "It's wood, trust me."

She felt bad then. Elias was older than either of them and

obviously not in the best shape. She held out a hand toward the crate and rubbed her fingers together as Elias stood up to his full height. *That should ease his load,* she thought.

"You guys got it?" she asked.

"It's solid, but not so bad now that we have it balanced," Elias said.

Hattie smiled inwardly, glad she could give them a hand without having to help them lift the rather unwieldy crate and risk a second splinter for the day. She hated using her magic in front of mortals, but the two men were oblivious, one still trying to place her and the other focused only on his work.

"So you're turning the old Stark home place into some sort of shop?" Elias asked her.

"Stark place?"

He nodded. Freya, the mau, moved toward him; something that surprised Hattie. She watched as the cat crept around the counter and slunk up to him, putting herself between his legs to sit. Distracted by her, he said nothing and instead, reached a hand down to her, running a couple of fingers across the top of her head.

"I'm not familiar with them," Hattie went on. "I'm renting the house from the Chappell family. They were planning to bulldoze it, but I convinced them it still had some life left in it."

His eyes grew wide. "I don't know who's worse, them or that developer, Kent, what's-his-name, that moved down here a couple of years ago. They're all wanting to tear down these beautiful, historic, old homes." He shook his head and then explained, "For years before the Chappells' started gobbling up properties in the village, after the oil boom ended in the '70s, the

Starks' raised quite a large family in this little house. I can tell you all about it some time; if you're interested, that is?"

Hattie smiled and nodded.

He grinned back. "It's not official or anything, you understand, but I consider myself to be something like the local historian. Actually, I am the historian in my, uh, my official capacity with the Sertoma group." He shifted gears again. "What did you say you're putting in here?"

"Actually, I didn't. It's going to be an herb and essential oils shop, at least part time." She thought, speaking of it to a local for the first time, it sounded odd to her own ears, and she wondered how he'd take it.

"Ah. Good thinking! Morels in the spring?" He raised an eyebrow.

"I hope."

"Yeah, you never know what sort of season you're going to get out of those. You should do well, regardless, with the ginseng pickers in the late summer and early fall. You're too late for them for this year though...Still, the Amish can get you goods all summer long and into the fall too."

"That's the plan." She let slip with the catch phrase that had made her famous.

He eyed her then and waggled a finger at her. "I know you... or, at least, I know of you. You're Althea Dwyer, aren't you? You're on that show...uh..." He snapped his fingers in the air a couple times and shook his head as he wracked his brain for the name.

"No. You're mistaken. It happens a lot, but I just look like her."

"Come on," he said. "You can't fool me. I just don't buy it." He paused, then called out, "Crestview Crunks! That's the show!"

Her face colored a little, giving her away. She ducked her head, but he caught it anyway.

"I knew it. I never forget a face, even without the makeup

and lights of Hollywood. My wife is a big fan, bigger than I am, even. Besides, I'm used to looking closely at things."

She looked up at him and let out a little sigh. "You got me."

"Say something funny...please? Another one of your lines from the show?"

"That stuff is all scripted. I'm not really all that funny, myself."

He grinned at that. "Sure you are. But, I've got to ask, why on earth are you opening an herb shop in Morelville, of all places?" He gave her an odd look.

She spread her hands. "Let's just say my character got cut out of the script and I decided I had enough of Hollywood for a while."

"Wow, Althea Dwyer, right here! Can't believe they'd cut out someone as good as you."

"It's Hattie. Please, call me Hattie."

"Okay..." He trailed off, still shaking his head at his brief brush with fame.

Before she could say anything else, he gathered himself and told her, "It would thrill everyone at Sertoma to have you, a new businesswoman in town and all, and such a high profile one at that. You should come to our next meeting."

"I'll think about it, but no promises this time around. I have a lot to do to get this place up and running."

"It's next Tuesday night at 7:00. We meet at the Community Center. If you come, I can show you a copy of the history logs I keep for them."

CHAPTER 2-THEFTS

B ridget poured more of her special brew into Selma's cup.

Selma held out a hand to stop her when the cup was only half full. "It's wonderful, sweetie, but I don't need the extra caffeine today. I've already had more coffee than I should have had."

"It's herbal. There's almost no caffeine at all."

"You're sure?"

Bridget nodded.

Selma removed her hand and let her finish filling the cup. "I don't know how you make it, but I've had nothing quite like it. It's...it's. What am I trying to say? An eye opener of sorts, I guess. I felt a little tired and worn when I got here, and now it has me feeling refreshed."

"Good, good," Bridget said, as she placed the old kettle back on the stove. "That's what it's supposed to do. I sort of noticed you were dragging a bit. What has you feeling so worn out?"

"Maybe worn out was the wrong way to put it." Selma sipped her tea slowly, then put her cup down. She pulled at one of her salt and pepper curls as she stared off toward the side entry door.

"Something wrong, dear?"

Selma shook her head, bringing herself out of her reverie. "I'm worried—"

When she didn't continue, Bridget prompted her. "About what? Please, go on."

"I think someone's stealing from me."

"Stealing what?" A wave of her friend's hand when the side door opened, and Hattie crossed the threshold cut Bridget's query off

Bridget's black cat, Sookie, darted past Hattie and outside before the screen door closed, no doubt looking for Freya, her hunting buddy. As Hattie twisted out of Sookie's way, she eyeballed her aunt, then glanced over at Selma sitting with her lips pursed, staring off at the wall behind Bridget. "Did I interrupt something?"

Bridget looked at Selma. The other woman gave a brief nod.

Bridget held out a hand toward her slightly older friend. "This is my dear friend Selma Morrison. She was just telling me she thinks someone is stealing from her."

"Oh no; how awful!" Hattie said. "Are you all right? Have you called the police?"

Selma raised both hands as she turned her attention to Hattie. "I'm fine, but please, no police."

"What was taken, dear?" Bridget asked, her voice taking on a more soothing tone.

Hattie moved around the table and took the seat on the other side, opposite Selma, while the older woman grasped for the words to explain. The chair at the far end was empty. Her aunt hated for anyone to sit there. It had been her uncle's place until his passing.

"Money...well, coins. Some of my rarer coins, some pretty valuable ones have disappeared."

"You collect coins?" Hattie asked.

Selma bobbed her head twice, nodding. "For years."

"You're sure they're gone?" Hattie shot her aunt a look. Bridget didn't catch it, as she stared at her own fingernails, which she insisted on keeping painted a candy apple colored shade.

"I wasn't, but now I am. Last week, I thought I just mislaid a case the last time I got a bug in my craw about sorting and cataloging things. Now I see that it's really gone and several other coins that weren't with the ones in that case are too."

Bridget spoke up. "And here I thought it was just me and my forgetfulness."

Hattie's head shot back around. "I don't understand. You collect coins too?"

"Oh, I'm not nearly the collector that Selma here is, but I have a few things that have some value and a couple of them I'm sure are missing."

She reached out to Selma and placed her hand on her arm as the other woman set her teacup down with a shaking hand. "What's missing from yours, dear?"

"Well, I'd set certain coins aside for an auction that's coming up...had them locked up, but set apart from some others. I planned to sell them and donate the proceeds for the restoration of the old Baptist church that Faye and Chloe are heading up. They were mostly high-grade Morgan Silver Dollars minted in Carson City."

A puzzled look crossed Hattie's face.

"Nevada," her aunt explained to her. "They minted coins there for a brief time, starting back in the 1870s."

"Oh. So, they're pretty rare then, I take it?"

"Fairly, and valuable," Selma said. "I was expecting to make over $30,000 dollars at the auction."

"Whoa!" Hattie said.

Bridget shuddered. "Mine aren't worth near that much but they're Carson City coins too...how very odd."

"Hardly odd or a coincidence, I'd say." Hattie put in. "Sounds like a pattern to me."

"Your dime, Selma? What about it?" Bridget turned from Selma toward Hattie. "She has a Carson City dime that's also worth several thousand dollars."

"No; that's safely tucked away. I moved that to a safe deposit box at the bank after I had it graded and slabbed. I couldn't take a chance with it...with myself, that is." She dabbed at the corners of her eyes. "I don't know what to do now. I expected those Morgan dollars to bring a pretty penny, like I said. They were graded and slabbed too, and the auction buyers would have been all over them. With coins missing here too," she waved an arm around, "I...I just don't want to bring the police in on this."

"There, there, dear." Bridget patted her arm.

"Someone's casing homes and stealing. The police should be involved," Hattie reminded the two older women.

"No. No police," Selma said, again. "It'll just make it worse."

Hattie drew in a breath, crossed her arms, and huffed, "How do you figure?"

"Listen, I love Melissa Crane...think she's a great Sheriff... just what this county needed, but I don't want even her poking 'round my house. Whoever is doing this is local; someone who knows the two of us and what we have, at a minimum. If we start the police to poking around, that will alert them that there's more to be had."

Her logic sounded completely backward to Hattie, and she started to question it, but Bridget raised a hand to silence her. "We can't just let it go, Selma. I shudder to think of anyone coming in here and violating my home...taking my property. I agree we need to keep the appearance that we've caught on to the missing coins down to a minimum."

"That's not what she said," Hattie said, her irritation at being silenced creeping into her voice.

Bridget shot her niece a look. "But it's what she meant."

Selma interrupted their exchange. "There must be something we can do?"

Hattie rose, went to the china cabinet, and pulled out a cup. She carried it to the stove and poured some of Bridget's special brew into it then leaned back against the stove to sip it as she listened to the other two women debate over their dilemma.

"Do you have any thoughts on who might have somehow gotten access to them, dear?"

Selma shrugged and spread her hands. "Not a clue. Very few people know I collect coins, apart from you and a few good, and I dare say discreet, auctioneers."

"You don't think any of them are shady?" Bridget asked, her brow furrowed.

"I've done business with two of them for over twenty years and the third for over ten, so no. You?"

Bridget shook her head. "I don't have the foggiest. Until a few minutes ago, I thought I was just being absent minded about where I put the darn things."

The two women fell into silence and stared off at the walls, both lost deep in thought.

As Hattie looked on, Bridget finally broke their impasse. "Why don't we call Faye?"

Selma squinted at her. "Crane?"

"Yes. Her and that Chloe Rossi seem to be great at getting to the bottom of things."

"Faye is Melissa's mother, Bridget."

"I know, but I don't think she'd tell Mel. I think she'd keep

our confidence if we asked her. And all we'd really be asking her
to do is poke around a little and keep her eyes and ears open. It's
to her benefit…well, to the old Baptist church if she can help us
figure this out. I could call her; have her meet us at your house
tomorrow?"

Selma shook her head. "I just don't know about that."

"How about if I snoop around a little to see what I can find
out?" Hattie asked Bridget after Selma left. She waved a hand at
the sink where three teacups and a couple of saucers now rested.
A dish cloth rose into the air along with a cup. The cloth began
wiping the cup out. "I need to get to know people in the village,
anyway. I could play it off as curiosity or nosiness, don't you
think?"

Bridget shook her head. "I really don't think that's wise. First,
you don't have time. You have the shop to get up and running
and then you need to build that business, and besides, you need
to be careful. You almost cost yourself your power in Hollywood.
Here in the village, you need to use it around mortals only as
absolutely necessary, and even then, think twice."

"I wasn't talking about using my magic. I was talking about
asking a few well-placed questions here and there. And, I promise, I'll be careful."

Bridget pointed at the creamer jug and waggled her fingers
in the refrigerator's direction. The door opened and the little
porcelain piece floated inside. "I don't suppose I can stop you,
can I?"

Hattie didn't answer her.

The matronly woman sighed. "Everything else aside, you
really ought to consider your future."

"My future? That's what I'm doing with the shop—"

Bridget shook her head at her niece again. "I mean...how to put this? Your full future. Don't you want a family, and kids, and—"

"Maybe someday...kids." Hattie said, cutting in.

"Well, if you want kids, you're going to have to find yourself a nice warlock and settle down. Or settle down so you can find yourself a nice warlock."

Hattie half turned away from her aunt and rolled her eyes.

Bridget called the younger woman out. "Don't think I don't know what you're thinking right now. You know it needs to be a warlock...or...or, even a mage, if you want to have any hope of being able to use your power and pass it on to your children. You marry a mortal, and you can forget all of that."

Hattie turned fully to her aunt then. "Trust me, marriage - to anyone - is the last thing on my mind right now."

CHAPTER 3–FAYE AND CHLOE

Morelville General Store
Tuesday, September 20th
Morelville, Ohio

"Do you have any fresh dinner rolls up here?" Selma asked Chloe. "If not, I'm going to have to go back and see what Hannah's got in the bakery."

"I think Marco sold the last of them just before he left for his fishing hole, but no need for you to run back there. I'll go back and get them," Chloe said. "I'll just be a minute." She left her position behind the cash registered and headed down the aisle toward the back of the store.

Selma glanced over at Faye who was busy at the slicer, churning out a mound of thinly sliced turkey breast. "I hope that's not all for me," she said. "I only wanted a half pound."

Faye smiled. "Actually, most of it's for me; or for Jesse, I should say. He's bailing hay for Roy, on out the road over the next couple of days since he broke his leg and can't do for himself. He's going to come in at lunchtime and grab it. I'll just be another sec."

"No rush. Take your time. I've got nothing but time."

Faye glanced at the slightly older woman. She'd known Selma over thirty years. Something didn't seem right with her. She stopped the slicer and piled a little of the meat on the scale next to it. "Just a smidgen over half a pound."

"That's fine. Just fine."

"Anything else besides those dinner rolls?"

"No. That should do it."

Faye jumped in, her concern for the woman spilling over. "Something on your mind?"

"No...no, nothing. Why do you ask?"

Faye smiled again. "Sweetie, you look as though you're carrying the weight of the world on your shoulders."

Selma shifted side to side on her feet, then put her hands down on the counter to stop herself. "Let me ask, how's the restoration planning for the old Baptist church coming?"

"Honestly? We're sort of at a dead stall until we can raise some more funds."

Selma's face fell. "I was afraid of that. How much do you think you'll need to get going again?"

"Well, let's see," she said, then turned at the sound of footsteps coming from the back. "Ah, here's Chloe with your rolls and it looks like a few more bags for up here to boot."

"Talking about me?" Chloe called back.

"Selma was just asking about the church restoration."

When Chloe reached the counter, she put one bag of rolls down in front of Selma and then stepped across the aisle and placed the others into an empty spot on the shelf next to the commercially made bread. "It's not going as well as we had hoped," she said, answering for Faye, as she rearranged the shelf. "Frankly, we're tight on funds. The building owner claims to not have a dime to spare. The only donations we've had besides our own sweat equity and what we could spare so far have been small ones, here and there. We need to raise a few thousand dollars just to put the roof back to right, for starters."

Selma clucked her tongue. "Jason should help more. Myself, I was baptized in that church and later married there. It breaks my heart to see it in the condition it's in. I'm glad you're doing this, and I'd like to donate what I can. It won't be a lot, I'm afraid. A few hundred dollars, for now."

Chloe clasped Selma's arm. "That's very generous of you. We can do quite a bit with that."

"I want to make a much larger contribution, but I just can't do as much as I hoped."

Faye sensed that there was more to the story. "What's wrong dear?"

The front door opened. All eyes turned to see Hattie coming in, carrying a bakery box from Hannah's. Looking at Selma, she said, "I thought it was you I saw in here."

"Yes, yes." Selma looked at Faye and Chloe. "Have either of you met Bridget's great niece, Hattie?"

Chloe extended a hand as she eyed the younger woman up and down. "I haven't, but Marco, my husband, mentioned you... said you're the one renovating the inside of that old house down the street. He said he thought you looked just like Althea Dwyer. I must say, you do."

"You might as well tell them," Selma said. "It's a small village. Why, I'm surprised word hasn't gotten out already."

"What word?" Faye asked. "What am I missing?"

Hattie blushed. "My real name is Hattie Novak. I grew up in Zanesville. My stage name...screen name, I should say, is Althea Dwyer. I'm an...an actress."

"Oh," was all Faye managed.

"Faye Crane! I can't believe it!" Chloe was giddy. "For once, I know something, or at least I picked up on something, before you did."

Faye gave a half shrug, then smiled at Hattie. "Sorry. I'm not up on all the latest television. What shows have you been on?"

Chloe couldn't help herself. "She's on that sitcom your grandchildren love, Crestview Crunks." She clasped Hattie's hand again. "Faye's granddaughter Beth is just going to be all over herself, wanting to meet you. How long will you be in town? I mean, shouldn't you be - what do they call it? Taping? No, wait! That's the old-fashioned term. Shouldn't you be recording the show right now?"

Hattie smiled and nodded as she pried her hand out of Chloe's grasp. "How are you today?" she asked Selma instead of responding to Chloe, her concern clear.

Faye, happy for the change of subject said again, "Yes, you seem out of sorts. Anything we can do?" She pointed to Chloe and then back to herself.

Selma blew out a breath. "Bridget suggested yesterday that I talk to the two of you. Since I'm here, I might as well." She put her purchases back down on the counter and told them about her missing coins while Hattie collected a few things from the shelves, within earshot of the other three women.

Faye and Chloe listened silently, just nodding at first.

When Hattie returned to the counter, Selma turned to her. "You might as well tell them the rest."

"There's more?" Chloe asked.

"Yes. Aunt Bridget also has coins missing and, that's not the half of it, hers are all Carson City Mint coins too."

Chloe looked at Faye. "That's not a coincidence."

Faye shook her head no.

"Somebody was targeting those coins who knew the two of you had them. That's obvious," Chloe said.

Faye nodded her agreement. She addressed Selma, "Who knew about your collection?"

"That's just it," Selma said, spreading her hands. "we talked about that yesterday and then I pondered on it most of the night. My late husband, God rest his soul, knew of course. And then there are three different auctioneers I deal with, and that I trust. I've been doing business with all of them for years, but then there's also everyone at all those auctions. There are people that are regulars at the auction houses I go to that recognize me and know what I buy. I mean, I try to keep to myself, but I'm not the only coin collector that goes to those things. I always have people bidding against me, and it's usually the same people."

"Ever brought any of them to see your collection?" Chloe asked.

"Heavens, no! Besides, two of the auction houses are out of state and one is over two hours from here."

Faye rubbed her arms as she asked, "Do you think any of them are aware of where you live?"

Selma thought for a minute. "I suppose it's possible. Anyone standing around while I was signing up for a bidder number might have got a glimpse of my ID or my paperwork." She rubbed her neck. "Lordy, they all have multiple worker bees that help at those things, too. Who knows who has access to what at those places, now that I think about it?"

"Sweetie," Faye spoke softly, "It sounds like this is a matter for the police. Why, it could be one of dozens of people, and folks from out of state, to boot. That would probably fall under the FBI, even."

"Yes," Chloe said, agreeing. "This might involve some sort of major theft ring."

"Here's the thing," Hattie began, before Selma could say anything else. "Aunt Bridget didn't get her coins at auctions. None of them. She told me she inherited most of them and mail ordered the rest. So, no auctioneering crews or their clientele figure into the thefts of her stuff."

"Hmm," Chloe said. "Then it really is a puzzle." She glanced over at Faye.

Faye stifled a grin. "I see that look Chloe Rossi! You want to take this on, don't you?"

Chloe shrugged. "If we can get her, her coins back, she can still auction them." She glanced at Selma, who nodded her confirmation, "and use some of that money to help with the restoration. I don't see Jason stepping up with any sort of money anytime soon."

Selma harrumphed at that. "I don't like to speak ill of anyone, but that man is the very definition of a tightwad. Why he even bought that building is beyond me."

"Think, Selma," Faye asked. "Is there anyone else at all, anyone local who might know about what you've got?"

"I used to do a lot with Delores Chappell before she went to the pokey for smuggling. She was the only one that knew about my stuff, her and Bridget, anyway, or so I thought. There wouldn't be anything those hooligans in her family could find of mine at her place, though. Frankly, whoever it is knows exactly what they're taking. They're only taking the Carson City currency coins in near mint to mint condition. None of my other currency or any of my commemorative coins are missing and nothing below the grade of an eight got taken."

"Grade?" Chloe asked.

"A professional coin grading service graded and slabbed almost most of my coins. Well, a lot of the more recent ones I purchased that way. Others I purchased in the past ungraded I've had done. That's the only way to establish their value."

"Who grades them for you, Selma?" Hattie asked, the wheels turning in her head.

"Most I bought that way from the auction houses but, over the years, Elias Penny has done a few for me. He's an alum from one of those coin grading companies or the other. There are two big ones, and I can't recall which. Anyway, it's been quite some time since the last one though. Buying ungraded stuff is pretty risky, anymore."

Hattie chuckled. "I just met Elias yesterday...different. His name fits him, I see."

"Oh," Selma waved a hand. "He's a harmless sort. A lot of bluster and a bit of self-importance in his demeanor, but he means well."

"Can I ask, Selma," Faye said, "were your coins insured?"

"No. Well, not specifically, anyway. I suppose to have them covered under the household contents clause of my insurance, I'd have to dig through my purchase records and get with Elias to see if he kept any records himself, then file a police report. That puts me back at square one. I just don't want to do that."

Faye's brow furrowed. "I don't understand."

"No offense dear, but I just don't want your daughter or any of her deputies crawling around my house, looking at stuff, cluing whoever it is in, that I'm aware stuff is missing or that there may be more there that is of value." She smiled at Chloe, shaking her head, "I don't even want your daughter to know because, as good of an investigator as she seems to be, she's bound to say something to Melissa or involve her somehow."

"Don't be too sure about that," Chloe cautioned her. "Dana could be a big help here and she wouldn't say a word to Mel if we asked her not to."

Faye cleared her throat. "We shouldn't be encouraging lying, even by omission, between—" The sound of a vehicle in need of a new muffler going up the State Route out in front of the store interrupted her. The front windows vibrated at the sound. "When is he going to get that thing fixed?" She threw her hands up, leaving her question hanging in the air.

"Who is that?" Hattie asked as she watched the old beater pickup truck pass by the windows going west, out of town. "I saw him down by my shop the other day, as I was on my way down there."

"Blake Wagner," Faye said.

"Bad news," Chloe said. "Stay away from him, if you can help it."

Selma slapped her fingertips onto the counter. All eyes turned to her as she said, "I've just thought of something!"

CHAPTER 4–STICKING THEIR NOSES IN

"Blake would know I have coins. Not necessarily what I have, but that I have them," Selma said.

"Pardon? How on earth would he know? Does he collect them too?" Faye asked.

Selma shrugged. "Not that I'm aware of, no. Could be, though."

"So, I'm confused," Hattie said. "Who exactly is he, and how would he know?"

Chloe and Faye both started talking at once. Faye deferred to Chloe. "Like we said," she began, "he's bad news. He's a local gunsmith and all-around ne'er-do-well who seems to pop up every single time there's anything at all wrong anywhere around here."

Faye simply nodded.

"I hope to the high heavens," Chloe continued, "that, for your sake, he's not involved in this because, if he is, I'm sorry, but I want no part of it."

"I'll second that," Faye put in. "You really should talk to the police, if that's the case." She paused, thinking for a moment, then asked, "Why on earth does he even know about your collection?"

Selma sighed. "Blake did some work on some guns Joe bought for next to nothing at that big Swappers Day affair they have over there in Licking County. This was, as I recall, a couple or three years ago, just before Joe passed. He brought them over to the house when he was done with them to go over them with Joe. I was sorting through the previous night's auction haul in the den. Joe brought him in there to show him something or other in his gun cabinet."

"Two or three years ago?" Hattie asked. "It seems unlikely he's the thief after all this time, don't you think?"

Faye interjected, "I wouldn't put anything past him."

Selma's face fell.

Chloe took pity on her as she watched her gather her purchases up again. "We'll do a bit of poking around, discreetly of course, dear, and see if we can find out anything useful at all."

Selma nodded her acceptance, bid them all goodbye, and left.

Hattie opened her wallet and took out some money to pay for her purchases. While Chloe rang her up, she said to the two women, "I'll help you look into this in any way that I can. It's the least I can do. You've both been so nice about this, about looking after Aunt Bridget and certainly after her friend."

"That's very kind," Faye said, "but I'm not sure there's anything we can do. We'll probably have to talk to Selma a bit more before we decide if we can do anything. Who knows, she may find her coins. She has a habit of misplacing things."

As Hattie left, she thought to herself, '*If Aunt Bridget couldn't find something, she'd just use her magic to put it back in its place if it was in range. Those coins are gone.*'

"I don't know what to make of that, Hattie," Faye said to Chloe.

"What do you mean?"

"Can't quite put my finger on it, but she gives me a bad feeling."

Chloe crinkled her eyes as she looked at Faye. "Really? I don't get that kind of vibe from her at all."

"Vibe?"

"A feeling, like you said."

"My hair stands up a little when she's around." She rubbed an arm with her other hand. "That's the kind of 'vibe' I get."

"Not me. I feel like she has a good aura around her."

"Vibes? Auras? Next thing I know, you'll be telling me you believe in magic and witchcraft!"

"I do believe in witchcraft."

Faye leaned back a bit and gave her friend a look. "Aren't you Catholic? I mean, I know you go to church with me now but... but Catholics don't believe in that stuff."

"But we believe in miracles? How is magic different? Besides, I believe in a lot of things the Catholic Church doesn't necessarily approve of."

"Come on! Everyone knows magic is fake...all tricks. Miracles are...miracles are acts of God."

"Magicians are performers. They're doing tricks. Witches are real. I'm sure of it."

"And you think Hattie is a witch?"

"She could be. The powers that be in Hollywood seem to think so."

"What are you talking about?" Faye asked.

"I guess you wouldn't know, since you didn't even know who she is. Actually, I played that part off while Hattie was here because I didn't want to embarrass her." Chloe leaned closer to her friend and whispered, "The rumor is her contract didn't get renewed for the Crestview Crunks' show. There were rumors going 'round that she's a witch or a Wiccan and she was casting spells to tray and further her acting career."

Faye fluttered a hand toward the magazine rack. "You need to stay away from those tabloids."

Chloe shrugged. "Believe what you want, but let me ask you this; haven't you ever had visions or premonitions, yourself?"

The other woman was quiet for a minute. When she spoke, her words came out as a question. "What made you ask me that?"

"I can feel that in your aura. It's faint, but it's there."

As she nodded slightly, Faye admitted, "When I was a child, I could see things...I had premonitions, as you called them. Mom didn't believe me, but my grandmother did. Mom always said I was just nosy, sticking my nose in where it didn't belong, and then having dreams about what I overheard later."

"Do you believe that's what happened?"

Faye rubbed her hands up and down her forearms. "I don't know what to believe. That was a long time ago. I don't have them anymore. Haven't for years."

Chloe sensed she was holding something else back. "What?"

Faye couldn't look at her friend.

"You don't, but someone does, don't they?"

She gave in because she knew Chloe wouldn't drop it. She drew in a deep breath and said, "Beth," as she let the air escape in a huff. "Kris thinks they're just bad dreams. Neither of my girls had them...the visions. Seems like it skips generations." She looked away again, staring off at the wall across from where she stood.

"We don't have to talk about it, not now, if you don't want to," Chloe said.

Faye changed the subject. "What we really need to talk about is how we're going to get this restoration going with no big donor commitments. I didn't say anything about it while Selma was here, so I didn't embarrass her, just like you didn't want to embarrass that Hattie, but the word was that she was going to give us several thousand dollars for the project; maybe more. Not now though, so now what do we do? Jason is just so tight with a nickel. Why, he's probably not going to lift one finger or donate a single cent to this, but I'm sure he's going to want to benefit from it in multiple ways."

"How is it he even owns the property?" Chloe asked. "You never told me."

"He doesn't; not all of it, anyway. He only owns the structure. The township owns the land the church sits on."

"That's an odd arrangement."

"It's because of the water well and the plumbing. The church only had a hand pump well outside as late as the 1970s. It ran dry; needed dug deeper. They couldn't afford to pay for that, let alone to run plumbing to the building like the state was demanding. They sold the land out from under themselves to the township for a dollar," Faye said, "then the township put in the new well and paid to run the pipes in. The church added indoor plumbing over time and paid the township pocket change in rent for over twenty years on the land."

"Why would the township do that?"

"Nobody knows, exactly," Faye said. "Being neighborly, I guess."

"So, when did Jason buy the building?"

"About a half-dozen years ago, after it had been vacant since the church folded in '92." Faye held up a hand. "Before you ask, I haven't got a clue what his ultimate plans are for it beyond what he's committed to letting us do with it."

"Sounds like it's a good thing we got it all in writing."

Faye gave a half toss of her head. "There's likely some truth in that."

"So, if we know we won't get anything out of him, what are you thinking about trying to help Selma?"

"I'm thinking," Faye said, "that I really don't want to tangle with Blake, like you said to her, and that's what this looks like to me. It has Blake Wagner written all over it."

"What would he want with a bunch of old coins though, valuable or not? He's all about living off the land and such," Chloe said.

"True. That, and being a lackey for Kent Gross." Faye was quiet for a few seconds. "He might sell them for money or melt them down for their metal content for something. Now that I could see him doing."

"I never thought about that," Chloe said. "The metals in those old coins could be pretty valuable too and untraceable once they're melted."

Faye shook her head hard. "That hardly seems right, though. Think about it; whoever is doing this seems to take only Carson City Coins. They're not taking anything else that might have silver in them or high copper content or anything like that."

"True."

"Maybe we should close up here and go out to Elias Penny's place...pick his brain a bit about these coins."

'That's the spirit!' Chloe thought.

"Coffee?" Mildred Penny offered. "I just made a fresh pot."

"Oh, no thank you," Faye declined while Chloe waggled a hand sideways.

"We just closed the store," Chloe told the woman as she directed them to overstuffed chairs in a book lined room. "We're not interrupting dinner, I hope?"

"No. Not really. I'm in the middle of preparations."

"We apologize," Faye said. "We're actually here to chat with Elias for a few minutes and we really shouldn't be long at all. Is he here?"

Mildred nodded. "He's in his study. Let me just let him know you're here."

When she left, Chloe stood again and looked around. "I would have thought of this room as a study, of sorts. It's dark, but there's definitely a den feel to it. Ever been in here - in this house - before?" she asked Faye.

"It's been a while but, yes, a couple times. Why?"

"No reason. It's not quite what I expected, is all."

"He's a very academic sort. You'll see."

Chloe bent slightly to inspect the spine titles on a shelf below shoulder height; all coin related. The next shelf over held volumes of Ohio history. As she looked up at the higher shelves, she felt, rather than heard, Elias enter the room and she turned.

His smile toward her seated friend was broad. "Why Faye Crane; what a pleasure to see you. What brings you out here?" He walked over to her, his hand extended. Mildred hovered in the doorway, neither in nor out of the room.

"Nice to see you too, Elias. Do you know Chloe? Chloe Rossi?" Instead of taking his outstretched hand, she swung an arm in Chloe's direction.

Elias half turned in Chloe's direction and moved toward her instead. "You run the store, right?"

Chloe nodded. "Yes, so to speak. We...my husband Marco and I, actually own it."

"That's right, that's right," he said, nodding. "I've only been in there a time or two since old Sheila...Well, anyway, only once or twice recently. You were busy with others on those visits. We're a little way out of the village, as you can see. Sometimes it's just easier for us to go on into Philo when we need a few things."

His little speech made, he extended his hand to her, and she took it and shook it briefly.

"You've got quite the collection here," she said, as she pulled her hand away and swept it to one side, indicating the expanse of shelves she was standing in front of.

"Den's the same way. Mildred and I, we're both big readers; not much into television, either of us." He looked away his words trailing off. After a moment, he looked from Chloe back to Faye. "So how can I help you ladies?"

"Just some insight, Elias," Faye said. "About coins. I understand you grade coins for people?"

He tilted his head, a quizzical expression on his face, as he took a seat opposite her after Chloe had seated herself. "I used to. I worked for NGC, the coin grading company, for a time, but I left there several years back."

"Oh," Chloe said. "We thought you were independent, I guess."

"I was after I left them, for a bit. I'm almost completely retired now. Keep my certification up though to keep my skills sharp. I still go to the shows to have a look around, see what's out there and to needle my old colleagues that are still in the business."

"You don't collect coins yourself?" Faye asked.

"No. I just go to see what's what." He chuckled. "I bet you're thinking that's strange?"

At their nods, he continued, "It's sort of like the carpenter whose house is in disrepair kind of thing. You know what I mean?"

Chloe nodded her agreement, getting his point. "One of my sons is a network engineer. People are always asking for help with their computers and he's the same way. Why, they can't even get him to run upgrades on his own cell phone."

They all laughed at that, but then Faye steered the conversation right back to coins. "You said you're 'almost' retired. So, you do, do some grading from time to time?"

"I haven't freelanced, per se, in four or five years now, but from time-to-time old Lucy Sharpe takes in a coin or two at her antique shop. I'll grade them and slab them for her, help her out, and keep my hand in the game." He paused as he looked back and forth between them. "May I ask? Why all the curiosity? Something you need me to look at?"

"Selma Morrison stopped by the store today," Faye began. "She told us you'd graded coins for her in the past."

He tilted his head up and pulled in his lower lip, thinking, then looked back at Faye as he shook his head. "It's been a while since the last time; Probably six or seven years ago. Might be longer. She was buying stuff she fancied, but she was getting some things she was paying top dollar for, and the quality just wasn't there. I advised her to look at only graded and slabbed pieces. Be sure she was getting what she paid for."

"Didn't that put you out of business?" Chloe asked.

He flipped a hand. "No one grades coins for the money. There's just not a lot of it at that end of the business."

Mildred guffawed at his remark. When they all looked her way, she blushed. "You'll have to excuse me. I need to check on dinner."

"Some coffee, please?" Elias asked. He watched his wife go, then leaned back in his chair and folded his arms. "So, are you wanting something graded? Is that what this is about?"

CHAPTER 5–CHATTING UP THE MONEY MAN

Faye realized she hadn't thought that far ahead. She shot Chloe a pleading look.

Mildred returned quickly with a carafe of coffee, giving Chloe precious seconds to concoct a story.

When Elias took his cup, then pressed her again, she began with, "My son's wife recently inherited a small collection from a relative of hers that passed on. She knows nothing about coins and none of them are, as you call them, slabbed. Not to my knowledge, anyway. She inherited a stack of coin books as well, but she knows nothing about quality or about the different mints or any of those such things. The more she tries to look things up, the more frustrated she gets."

If he noticed her hesitation or her nervousness, he didn't let it show. "You're looking for someone to grade everything for her?"

"I imagine," Chloe half shrugged, becoming more comfortable with her lie. "When I mentioned it to Selma, she mentioned you. I was hoping you could help, or at least steer me in the right direction."

Faye nodded along. Chloe's ability to make things up on the fly amazed her, but she tried not to let it show in her own face.

"I could look at them for her and give her some thoughts on what she should have looked at more closely. Do they live around here?"

"Oh...actually, no. They're in the Pittsburgh area; McKeesport. They're coming here for Thanksgiving, though." She bit her bottom lip at the deception.

"Mildred and I travel every year to her sister's place for the holidays, beginning with Thanksgiving. She can't get down here, you see." Mildred nodded in agreement, but she said nothing.

Chloe feigned disappointment.

Elias smiled at her. "Don't worry. There are a couple of very reputable dealers in the Pittsburgh area that I'm familiar with and that I can refer her to with every confidence. One can grade on site, and one will send things they feel are worth having graded directly to PCS for her, for a cost, of course."

"PCS?" Chloe asked. "I thought you said you worked for NGC?"

"I did. There's more than one grading company out there. PCS does a fine job too." He held up a finger. "I'll be right back."

The three women sat in silence until he returned moments later and handed Chloe a business card. "Give her my information, if you like. We can talk directly about what she has and I might save her some time and grief."

$\sim$

Tuesday Evening, September 20th
The Shanty
Morelville, Ohio

"Three Italian subs for Jesse and the kids; no onions on Beth's or Cole's, and a chicken club sub for me," Faye said.

Kasey rang up her order. "Kris working?"

Faye nodded. "And Lance is on the road...won't get back until later this evening. Those kids just won't stay at that house for a minute by themselves these days. You'd think it was haunted."

"Why don't they hang out over at Mel's place since she's right next door?"

"Mel'd make them work."

"And you and Jesse won't? Right!" Kasey laughed. "That'll be $26.50."

"Heavens, they better work for what it costs to keep them fed. I knew I should have put something in the crock pot this morning before I left. No offense, dear."

"That's probably why they want to be at the farm, Faye. They know Grandma will take care of them." She grinned and waved the order ticket. "I'll get this put in. It's going to be about ten minutes."

"Thanks. Is your husband around?"

"He just finished working on a compressor for one of the beer coolers...hasn't left yet."

"What kind of mood is he in?"

Kasey shrugged. "About as good as any other time. He just saved a bunch of money by being able to fix that himself so probably not too bad of a mood. Why?"

"I want to talk to him a little more about the Baptist Church restoration."

Jason Meyer came through the swinging kitchen door, working a damp, white kitchen towel over his grease-stained hands. She held back a shudder as she watched him look around the dining room until his eyes settled on her seated at a table near the front door where she could see the takeout order counter when her food emerged.

He sauntered over to her and addressed her without preamble. "Kasey said you want to talk about the church building."

"Yes."

"Look, if it's about money, I'll do what I can to help, but it won't be much. I already told you that. This place here is a black hole." He swung an arm wide.

Her eyes followed his arm, taking in the nearly full dining room in a pizza shop, in a tiny village, on a Tuesday night. She held her tongue. She needed his cooperation.

"That building is crumbling," he continued. "I'd like to see it restored and put to good use, but I don't know that it's worth saving. Hell, I don't know why I bought it in the first place. Don't know what I was thinking there."

"So, you didn't really have any plans for it yourself, at first?"

He looked away from her, shaking his head. "Not a one. Right after I bought it, I was using it for storage, but I learned really quickly that there are too many roof leaks over there for that."

Faye shuddered at the thought of the once beautiful little church being used as a repository for whatever junk Jason had seen fit to store there. "May I ask, if we get it back into order, what your plans are for it then? I mean, I don't think you've ever said why you've agreed to let us... me and Chloe, try this."

Jason looked away again and then back toward her, but he stared at the wall somewhere over her shoulder. "I haven't crossed that bridge yet, but I know this, it means a lot to lots of people in this town. Most of my family went to that church until I was a tot, anyway."

She wasn't convinced he was telling her the whole truth, but it was more than he'd ever said on the matter before.

As she left, she passed Kent Gross, the developer, on his way into the shop. She gave him a half smile and nodded politely but didn't speak to him. Whatever he was up to, hanging around inside the village on a Tuesday evening, she didn't want to know about.

She turned down Jamison, the next short street over from the store which sat on the corner of the State Route and Quinn Street and the bakery behind it that faced Quinn. The township trustees had named Jamison and Quinn streets after old oil boom families. The Jamison's were long gone in Village lore; but the Quinns remained. They had been generous with funds to restore the opera house, but a rough year for the family business left them tapped out to help with the church restoration project.

She drove slowly, stopping in front of the old church about halfway down. The church faced the street, its back to the back of the now nearly restored old opera house that faced Quinn like the bakery did. She knew there was at least an acre of land between the backs of the two buildings. Most of it was the plot owned by the township.

She let out a heavy breath. Every time she looked at the old church, she saw something else that needed done. Now she noticed a crack in the sandstone blocks of the foundation, under the front entry and belfry she hadn't seen before. That worried her as much as the condition of the roof.

"I just saw Faye Crane leaving here," Kent said to Jason. "Did she say anything to you?"

Jason shook his head and shrugged one shoulder. "Didn't talk to her. She was here to pick up food. I try to avoid her anyway because she's always wanting money for this and that."

"Fixing all the ills of that old church building, no doubt. You should just sell it to me and be done with it. I'd have her go pound sand."

"I told you I can't do that. It's historical. It means something to my mother, and my grandmother, you know?" He tried to raise an eyebrow. "You'll get to do what you want with it, and you won't have to put a cent in it. Neither will I. Wait. You'll see."

CHAPTER 6–BODY THE FIRST

Later Tuesday Evening, September 20th
The Crane Family Farm
Morelville, Ohio

"Althea Dwyer, right here in Morelville? A celebrity? Wait until my friends here about this!" Beth gushed.

"What friends?" Cole asked, his tone teasing. "You know you don't have any!"

"Cole Roberts, we'll not have that at the dinner table. Now you apologize to your sister," Faye said to the sixteen-year-old.

"Yes ma'am. Sorry." He mumbled the last bit in Beth's direction as he took a big bite of his sub.

"When can I meet her? Do you think she'd give me an autograph?" Beth bounced around in her chair in her excitement, her own sub untouched.

"You gonna eat that?" Cole asked as he reached for it.

Jesse Crane reached out and gave his grandson's hand a quick slap. As Cole jerked the offending hand away, Jesse told him, "You know she will. She eats just as much as you."

"Her real name is Hattie," Faye said, "and she's no different from anyone else around here." To herself, she thought, '*except maybe that she's stirring a little trouble for some older folks that don't need any.*'

Jesse shook his head. "I don't see what the big deal is, either."

"She's on TV, Grandpa!" Beth said.

"Yeah; so?" Jesse knew who the actress was, but he liked to tease his granddaughter.

Cole couldn't hide his own interest any longer. "She's on Crestview Crunks, Grandpa...only the funniest show ever!"

"As funny as Hogan's Heroes?" Jesse asked, hiding a grin.

Beth rolled her eyes. "Grandpa, really? That old show? Seriously!"

The Wee Hours, September 21st

Beth sat bolt upright in her bed and screamed in terror. The sound split the night in the tiny house. Moments later, her mother and her stepfather both burst into her room. Lance flipped on the overhead light while Kris charged past him for the bed. She sat down and took her daughter into her arms.

"That old woman is dead."

"What old woman? What did you see?" Kris asked her.

"The one that lives just across from Aunt Mel. That one. It's terrible...a big mess."

"Across from Mel?"

"Yeah." She sobbed and swiped at her eyes with the sleeve of her pajama top. "The one that never comes out of her house except to get her mail. She does that thing with the stamper."

"Stamper?" Lance asked.

Kris looked at Lance and then back at her daughter. "You mean, Delores, the notary?"

Beth just nodded.

"Honey, she's in jail, remember? She's been there..." Kris thought for a few seconds. "Well, it has to be a year and a half or more now."

Beth shuddered. "She's...she's not home? In her house, I mean?"

"No baby, no."

"It was just a dream?"

Kris pulled Beth close and hugged her. "Yeah, baby. Just a dream."

∾

Late Morning, Wednesday, September 21st
Morelville, Ohio

Faye and Chloe stood on the sidewalk, out in front of the village post office, staring down the street toward a small house, several doors down and around a corner, only part of the back side visible from their vantage point. The corner of the block was ringed with police vehicles, their blue lights flashing. The rescue squad from the volunteer fire house was there, lights flashing, too.

"I thought that house was empty?" Chloe questioned Faye.

"It was. It is," Faye said. "That's where Delores Chappell lived; the one who's in jail over that whole smuggling deal Dana was all mixed up in when she was still with Customs. The family has had it all closed up for a while now."

"Dana cracked that case," Chloe said.

Faye reminded her, "With Mel's help."

"It's not worth arguing over, Faye." She changed the subject. "I wonder who's in there?"

"Probably one of the Chappell clan," Molly, the Postmaster

said, as she came out of her building to check on all the commotion and overheard Chloe. "They check on the place all the time."

"Can't be Delores," Faye said again, for good measure. She glanced over her shoulder, back toward the store. Marco was standing outside now too, his work to fix a broken door hinge on a display case abandoned.

As the three women watched, Hattie stepped off the porch of the Chappell owned house she was slowly turning into a shop, and glanced up at the sign installer working slowly on the porch roof as he watched the events unfolding further down the street. She looked away from him and craned her neck to the right to see what she could see for herself of the going's on just around the corner. She half turned and glanced up the street to her left. Spying the three women, she walked toward them. Freya hopped down off the porch rail and followed her at a distance.

She spread her hands as she got closer. "Anyone know what's happened?"

"We were going to ask the same of you," Molly answered for all of them.

"I don't have a clue. I was on the phone with a fixtures supplier when the ambulance went screaming by the front windows over there and then squad cars started going by."

A man walked from around the front side of the house to the side of it that ran parallel to the State Route that ended in the village. He looked at the emergency vehicles arrayed along the side of the road and then up the street toward them. As he waited, and they all watched, the coroner's old hearse rolled slowly past them, toward the melee.

Chloe shot a look at Faye and then looked back at the scene spread out before them. "Who's that guy down there waving toward the guys in the hearse?"

Molly leaned forward and peered down the street as if she

could see better. She shook her head. "I think it's old Stanley, himself."

"Stanley who?" Chloe asked.

Faye had a look of disbelief on her face. "I think you're right," she said to Molly. Turning to Chloe, she told her, "I doubt you know him. It's Stanley Chappell, Delores' dad. He's got to be ninety something, or nearly a hundred. You rarely see him out and about, and certainly not down here in the village."

"I'm renting my shop space off of the Chappells, and I've never met him," Hattie chimed in.

As they watched the coroner unload a gurney out of the back of the hearse, a County Sheriff's Department SUV came down the highway too.

Faye waved at her daughter as she drove by their little group, but Mel didn't acknowledge her. She stared straight ahead at the scene spread out before her.

"Do you think Mel will tell us what's happened?" Chloe asked.

Faye shrugged. "That's doubtful. She's pretty tight-lipped about stuff. You know that. Besides, we already know what happened. Someone's dead."

"Yeah," Molly said, "But not who or how."

CHAPTER 7–MORELVILLE GRAPEVINE

Jesse Crane stood outside the store at the corner with Marco and a couple of other men, across the side street from the group of women that included his wife.

Elias Penny walked out of the bakery that occupied space behind the store. Seeing the cluster of men just standing there staring down the street, he walked over and joined them.

Jesse nodded his way. "Elias. Ain't seen you 'round in a while."

As he dipped his head in acknowledgment, Elias replied, "My mother was very ill. Mildred and I were taking turns tending to things here and tending to her over in Duncan Falls. She didn't want to leave her house."

"Don't blame her," another man said as he walked up to the group. He looked down the street at all the flashing lights. "Anyone know what's going on?"

"Search me, that's for sure," Jesse said. "Looks like they're working on something at Delores Chappell's old place. I suppose word will get around soon enough, though."

Chloe Rossi left Faye, Molly, and Hattie standing where they were and walked back toward the store. As she approached the men, she heard Elias talking.

"Chappell, huh? Well, I know she was a collector. If they find coins down there, the police better lock that place up tight. Every collector and crook for miles around will want to dig into that."

Jesse gave him an odd look. "Ain't you interested yourself? Ain't you a dealer?"

"Retired. Long retired," he answered as he glanced around at all the men in the group. "I admit, I'd be curious to see what she has. I really don't know her except in passing. Every now and again, I run into her at the post office. She did notary work, didn't she?"

"She did before she went to jail," Jesse said. "She's been in prison for better than a year. Far as I know, she still is but, even if she was out, I imagine the license to do that gets revoked when you're a convicted felon."

"It would hardly seem like that would pay enough to be much of a collector of anything, especially coins," Elias said.

Chloe skirted around the group of men and entered the store.

"Notary work pays nothing at all," Jesse was saying as the door closed behind Chloe. "Didn't you hear me? She was a convicted felon. Had a whole other racket going on. Where were you when all of that went down? Maybe you ought to buy a paper and move closer to town." Marco and the other men chuckled at Jesse's gruffness.

"I guess I missed it. I must have been tending to my mother or something, God rest her soul."

Jesse grew quiet and hung his head, contrite, but Marco couldn't help not getting a jab in. "My condolences on the death of your mother but, I've got to say, I'm a, quote, 'outsider' and I knew all about that."

Jesse raised his head then and guffawed at that. "You didn't even live here then. Your daughter headed up the investigation. That's how you knew."

Chloe's feet ached. Closing time had come and gone a half hour before. She longed to go home, put her feet up and relax for a bit, but the village had been abuzz all afternoon about Delores being home from jail and now found dead. It seemed to her and Marco like the store had become a hub for all the town gossip.

The two of them hustled around the small space, ringing up people who were actually buying things and trying to move the ones who just wandered in to get the latest scuttlebutt along.

"It was that gang she was wrapped up in," Jason Meyer was saying, above the din. "I'm telling you. Someone in that gang killed her. Mark my words!"

Meyer was standing, blocking the aisle in both directions, two feet in front of the register. Chloe shot Marco a look and held it, then tipped her head toward Jason when he finally took notice.

Marco stepped over to the register and called out, "Who's next? Can I help you there, Jason?"

"Uh...yeah. Uh...sure."

The notorious tightwad grabbed a pack of gum off a rack and winced when Marco said, "That'll be $1.19."

As he dug through his pockets for change, he quizzed the storekeeper, "When did she get out of jail? How long has she been back here in Morelville?"

Marco splayed his hands. "I really don't know. I've never actually met the woman. You've all reminded me several times today I'm not from around here."

"Don't feel bad," Craig Stroud said, commiserating with

Marco as he laid a loaf of bread on the counter. "You two aren't the only ones getting beaten up on today. People are starting to realize we have a celebrity in our midst."

"We do?" Jason asked. "Who?"

Stroud puffed out his chest, "I guess I get to be the first to tell you that Althea Dwyer is setting up shop down the road."

"Her name is Hattie Novak," Chloe said.

Jason's brow furrowed. "Who and who? I don't know either."

Marco laughed. "They're the same person. Althea is Hattie's stage name, I guess you'd call it. She's on a sitcom all the kids watch."

Chloe gave her husband a playful slap to the shoulder. "You're not fooling anyone. You love it too!"

"Whatever," Jason said, ignoring her antics. Turning to Craig, he asked, "You watch that stuff?"

Craig smiled. "Sometimes. It's good stress relief."

Jason opened the gum and popped a piece into his mouth, but he didn't move away from the register.

As Faye Crane wandered through the front door, Marco turned his attention to Craig. Holding up the bread, he asked, "Will this be all for you?"

Faye shook her head at the scene in front of her and called out to her friends, "I stopped because I saw you were still open. I wondered if you needed any help to close up?"

"Thanks for your help," Chloe said to Faye as they went out to their cars. "I didn't want to be rude, but they just kept coming in."

"You're welcome. I don't mind putting them in their places. Every one of them in there knew better."

With that, both women looked down the street. Mel's county SUV was still parked just off the state route, along the side of the Chappell house.

"She's still down there," Faye pointed out, shaking her head. "I hope she'll fill us in about what happened. I'm curious about how Delores got released from prison and why Mel hasn't said a thing about it. I figure she had to know a criminal she had a part in getting locked up, got released."

Chloe started to remind her it was her daughter Dana's case when she was with the Customs Service that landed Delores in the pen, but she bit her tongue. There wasn't any point in quibbling over it. Mel had been involved. She was asking Faye if she wanted to stop by for tea before heading home when the door to the post office opened and Molly walked out.

"She's in there awful late," Faye whispered. "Probably hung around town to be nosy."

Spotting them, Molly crossed the side street and joined them.

Faye jumped right in. "You're working really late, aren't you?"

"No...no. Actually, I left and went over to the house about my usual time. Had to come back in and reset my, uh...my scanner. Got a call from my POOM. It didn't download right."

"POOM?" Chloe asked.

Molly fluttered one hand. "The area operations manager." She looked back over her shoulder, down the street, and then turned back to the two of them. "What's the latest? You heard they found Delores dead in there, didn't you?"

Both of the other women nodded but said nothing.

"I heard," Molly went on, "they found her surrounded by coins from her coin collection."

Chloe looked at Faye, but she kept what she was thinking to herself in front of Molly. *Word moves fast around the village, but that has police knowledge only right now.*

Molly didn't notice Chloe's newly suspicious demeanor. Instead, she leaned in and confided, "I probably shouldn't say this, but I trust you two. If that's true about the coins, I'm going to have to tell the police, anyway. I know Delores has been collecting coins for a long time. The thing is, she was still getting coin catalogs and offers and even coins in the mail from sets she'd been collecting on subscription before she went to jail. Her family members would come and pick up her mail when they were in town here to tend to her house and yard and such. She was such a private person. I bet no one knows, besides them, that she collected coins. You know what that means?"

Chloe shook her head.

Molly said, "It means one of them might have killed her and taken some of her valuable stuff."

Faye waved a hand dismissively. "You don't know that. Heavens! She was an old woman!"

CHAPTER 8–WHAT FUNERALS TELL US

Old Stanley Chappell shuffled into the store. He looked at the register and smiled when he saw Faye. "I was hoping to find you in here."

"How are you today, Stanley?"

"Could be better, myself, but I'm certainly better off than my sister." He nodded at Chloe who was wiping down the slicer a few steps away.

"I'm so sorry for your loss," Faye said, as she dipped her head in deference. "We will miss Delores around here."

"As am I. My condolences," Chloe added.

"Thank you both. I appreciate that." He focused on Faye. "Even though we both know that's not necessarily true."

He braced his hands on the edge of the counter and worked his mouth as he gathered his thoughts. "I just want to quell some rumors going around. I know people come in here yapping. Let them know she was old. She had a heart attack, plain and simple. She was sitting there, in her home, enjoying her last moments on this earth and she died of natural causes."

Faye leaned toward him and reached out for his hand, covering it with hers. "I didn't even know she was...home, Stanley. Had I known, I could have been — I would have been looking in on her, making sure she was okay; that she had what she needed."

He took up her lead. "You're a good Christian woman. I just wish people in this town would have a little respect for the dead. The stories are flying."

"The best way to quell the rumors is to meet them head on. You can tell people exactly what happened at her memorial."

He pulled his hand away. "No funeral. No memorial. That's why I'm asking you for your help. They sent her–an old woman–to jail like a common criminal," he ground out. "This community seemed more than happy to see her go. I hardly think a funeral—"

Faye raised a hand to stop him, but spoke softly when she told him, "I didn't see it that way at all and I dare say many didn't. She was a member of this community for better than sixty years...longer than I've been on this earth. There are many people here who would want to pay their respects, not only to her, but to the family. A small memorial service would allow them to do that and allow you to stop the rumors." Faye flicked her eyes to Chloe, but she didn't chance turning and looking in her direction. *Her curiosity is rubbing off on me.*

He took a long time to think before responding, "I doubt she would have wanted one, but you're probably right."

"Sounds like he's going to have a service of some sort," Faye said to Chloe after the Chappell patriarch left.

"We have to be there," Chloe said. "You know as well as I do if she really was killed if it wasn't natural causes and it's over coins, there are no coincidences. They're all tied together."

"If what Molly said was true."

"Your daughter didn't deny it."

Fay sighed. "I know. I'd have to go anyway, since I agitated for the whole thing."

"I just have to wonder," Chloe went on, "where Molly got her information from last night. She doesn't live here in town. Mel and her folks weren't done down there when she came—"

Faye tossed a hand. "She's been the postmaster down here for years. She talks to everyone like she knows them. Before she came back last night, she could have talked to anyone."

"If that's true, then Mel or someone from her department let something leak. That, or Molly knows more than she should."

"Or it was wild speculation on her part. Something I wouldn't put past her either." Faye walked around the end of the counter toward the front door. "Are we getting a Milk delivery today?" she asked, changing the subject.

Late Saturday Morning, September 24th
Morelville, Ohio

Chloe wrinkled her nose. "It smells musty and like embalming fluid in here. And this line is crazy. I didn't think they used this little parlor anymore. It always seems dead over here, pardon the pun."

"Not since they built their new place in Zanesville," Faye whispered. "And, I dare say, not for a couple of years before that. Any funerals or memorials anyone wanted to have here in the village before that or instead of going all the way there since they got their new place, they had at the church."

"They've outgrown this. Why, it's nothing but a small house."

"Served them well for many years, though," Faye said. "But yes, it's too small to hold services in for anyone that's been around a while. I tried to tell Stanley..."

They entered the funeral home through a center hall entry-way. To their left was a cloakroom and the restrooms. To their right was a large opening into the back part of the only viewing room. They waited just inside the front door in a line that snaked into the viewing room and eventually up to the Chappell family arrayed on either side of a closed casket at the front of the room. There were chairs set up in the middle of the area for, perhaps, twenty people to sit. The line was two and three people thick along the outside wall to the right. Most people ignored the chairs.

A few minutes after they stepped through the front door, they shuffled forward to a position just inside the viewing room. Faye looked at the casket, still thirty feet and nearly as many people away. "It's closed."

"Why do you think they did that?" Chloe asked.

"Everyone who is anyone is trying to cram in here," Faye said, ignoring the question. Her eyes narrowed. "That Hattie is even here. She didn't even know Delores." She tipped her head toward the younger woman who was far nearer the casket in the line than they were.

Chloe said, "Nor did I. I moved here after she went to prison, remember? I've heard the stories, but I never met the woman. I'm here to pay respects to the family. Hattie is here with her aunt, whom I suspect has known Delores for years."

"I'll give you that one," Faye conceded the point.

Chloe leaned in and whispered, "I just remembered some-thing. Didn't Selma Morrison tell us she used to do things with Delores with coins?"

Faye's mouth dropped, but she closed it quickly. "That she did," she whispered back.

"Do you think Bridget ever had any friendly dealings with Delores?"

Faye played with the idea in her head for several long

seconds before saying, "I don't think so, but I don't rightly know. Both have been here many, many years, but they're several years apart in age. At least, I think they are."

"Don't look now," Chloe said as she touched Faye's arm. "Blake just came through the door behind us. He looks rather disgusted with the line."

"Oh, he's an impatient sort, that's for sure," Faye said. "The question is, why is even here? He wasn't related to Delores, and he had no dealings with her I'm aware of. He and the Chappells are not on the best of terms, either."

"We'll just have to keep our eyes open."

Ahead of them, Bridgett and Hattie reached the bier. They spoke to the family members standing to the right of the casket before passing along it, Bridgett laying a hand on it and brushing it lightly before moving on to speak with Stanley who was standing to the left.

The two women watched as Bridget moved on to a photo display while Hattie hung back and had a few words with Stanley, ending in her pulling him aside to speak more privately for several long seconds.

Faye shot Chloe a look. She was watching them, too.

Chloe whispered, "Didn't she say she'd never even met him?"

"She's digging for dirt, I bet, about what Mel and her crew found." *And I don't trust her.*

The line moved a little quicker. Ten minutes later they were exchanging condolences with Stanley's eldest daughter, a woman Faye barely knew. She was a couple of years younger than Faye and had left Morelville as fast as she could after high school. She didn't come back often. Only for weddings and funerals, Faye thought.

Old Stanley had spent years trying to take care of a large

horse farm on the edge of town with little to no help from his offspring and eventual heirs.

The two women stopped in front of the casket. Chloe muttered a few words Faye didn't catch then crossed herself as she'd seen her do many times. *Once a Catholic, always a Catholic.* Faye laid a hand on the bier for a few seconds and dipped her head, sending up a prayer in her own way.

They stepped away after that and gave their condolences to Stanley, but they didn't linger with him. As they worked their way through the groups who had already paid their respects but who were still in the room, looking at photos and chatting, Chloe spied Molly coming through the doorway at the far end of the parlor. The crowd was thinning a bit at that end, the line not so long or thick. People were chatting quietly amongst themselves, but in those subdued tones usually reserved for somber occasions. Molly stood in her place, not speaking to anyone.

Chloe pointed her out to Faye. "Look who else just showed up," she leaned toward her and whispered. "Speaking of people who really have no ties to the family or business with Delores."

Faye begged to differ. "She's served the village as the postmaster for years. She's dealt with her quite a bit, I dare say. But," she held out a hand, "there is the question of how she knew as much as she knew."

"I've got my eyes on her and on Blake," Chloe said.

They worked their way out into an anteroom where more pictures were on display, all of a much younger Delores Chappell. "At least," Faye said, "they don't have one of those infernal videos playing. She's been around a long time, but she was practically a recluse the last umpteen years. She didn't interact or take part in community events much at all since I can't tell you when."

"We know why that was," Chloe reminded her. She half turned so she could see back into the room they'd left. From her angle, she could see Stanley's back and the line leading up to the bier. She could also see most of the hallway that ran the length of the building outside the anteroom, though it was crowded with people. It wasn't an ideal vantage point, but it would have to do.

When Hattie turned from where she stood next to Bridget at a collage of pictures, she spotted them and started toward them. Faye chose that moment to excuse herself, saying, "I've got to use the ladies' room. I'll be right back."

Chloe was skeptical given the throng in that direction, but she shrugged. "I'll wait right here. Keep my eyes and ears open."

Hattie caught the last bit. "For what?"

Chloe asked, "Have you been to many funerals in your young life?"

"I'm older than you think," Hattie confided. "Nearly thirty."

"That didn't answer my question."

The younger woman thought a minute. "A few. Three. One for my grandmother. Gramps was gone a few years before that, but I was too young to remember it," she said, a sheepish grin forming on her face. "The others were for people I knew...er, knew of, in Hollywood. One was a producer on the show."

"Natural causes, all?"

Hattie shrugged. "As far as I know."

"Well," Chloe whispered, "that might not be the case here, which is why being here for the viewing is pretty much mandatory."

Hattie screwed up her face, letting her confusion show. "I don't get how they're related."

"For someone who was on TV, you sure must not have watched much of it."

"Um, no. No time."

"I think it holds true in real life, too. At least, that's what all the cops I know tell me; the criminals often show up at the funeral."

Movement inside the viewing parlor caught Chloe's eye. Blake was nearing the family and Molly was jumping the line to land next to him.

Chloe nudged Hattie with an elbow. "Case in point." She tipped her chin toward the pair.

"That guy with the scruffy goatee and the woman with him?"

"Shh. Yes. They're not together, at least, not as far as I'm aware of."

Hattie whispered back, "That's the post office lady, right? Molly?"

Chloe nodded. "And the other is the guy we've warned you about, Blake."

When the pair reached the receiving area, they made quick work of paying their respects and moved off to a corner of the anteroom as fast as they could weave through the crowd around the easels of photo collages. As the two women half turned for a better view, the two of them bent their heads together and spoke in very low tones, oblivious to everything going on around them.

"I just wonder what that's all about," Chloe whispered to Hattie. "Oh, to be a bug on the wall over there."

Jesse Crane wormed his way down the hallway and came up alongside Chloe who had forgotten all about watching in all directions. She jumped when he spoke. "Have you seen Faye? I thought she came with you."

"She did. She's gone to the restroom, I believe. I'll let her know you're here if you'd like to go in and pay your respects."

"No, it's fine. I'll just wait for her."

"We've already been in," Chloe told him.

"Line's pretty long." He took a deep, ragged breath. "Back to the door almost at the other end."

"It's actually better now, but yes," Chloe said. She looked her friend's husband up and down. He'd changed out of his farm gear into a pair of clean jeans and his good cowboy boots for the viewing, but something wasn't right. "You seem a little out of sorts. Are you feeling all right?"

"Fine. Fine. It's been a long day. Tried to get one last hay cutting in. Breathing in that stuff all day always does me in." He looked about again. "How long has she been gone?"

"How about I make myself useful and go see what's taking so long?" Hattie offered. "All these people, she probably got side-tracked."

"In this crowd, that'd be easy for her to do," Jesse said. "Far too easy."

Hattie worked her way out of the anteroom and through the throng in the hallway, reaching the restroom just as Faye emerged. "Hi there. Sorry, but your husband is here looking for you. I left him with Chloe."

"Thanks," Faye managed. She let out a small sigh. "I was hoping to leave. It's still a zoo in here and it's getting hot."

"They're still in that room at the end of the hall. Do you want to wait here while I get them?"

"No. Jesse will be mad if I don't go through the Chappell lineup with him. Let's go." She turned and took a few steps in the anteroom's direction with Hattie following behind her then paused and turned to face the younger woman who almost plowed into her. She held out her hands, fingers splayed, palms down and tossed her head back a bit, letting Hattie know someone Faye didn't want to notice her was nearby. Faye stood still after that; her neck cocked over.

Hattie recognized a classic eavesdropping posture when she saw one and stood quietly without trying to see past Faye at whom she had spotted.

Faye's heart raced. Just over her shoulder stood Elias Penny and his wife Mildred. She was so self-conscious after her foray with Chloe out to his house, she wasn't sure he wouldn't make assumptions about her reasons for being at the calling hours for Delores. On the other hand, she found it odd that he had come.

Mildred had been standing silently next to her spouse when she spotted them, hands folded in front of her waist, as Elias and Lucy Sharpe went back and forth about something. Faye saw her walk past her and Hattie, eyes on the crowd in front of her, until she reached the restrooms and entered the ladies.

As she continued to listen to the conversation that went on after Mildred's departure, she got the impression Elias had not delivered on something Lucy was expecting from him. They spoke in low tones, respectful of the dead and of the occasion, but even though she couldn't hear much, she could gather from the words she could pick out that Lucy was angry.

Faye put a hand on Hattie's shoulder and turned her in the other direction, whispering, "We'll go back the long way around."

They worked their way down the left side of the viewing parlor and out into the anteroom off the other end where Chloe and Jesse were making small talk with a couple of other mourners. Faye collected Jesse and went with him back the way she'd just come, right past old Stanley, and back to the end of the line.

Chloe, meanwhile, shrugged at Hattie. "At least you found her."

"Oh, we found out something on the way back, or...or at least, she did. She'll have to tell you about it. I could see on her face she thought it was important."

Intrigued, Chloe leaned toward her newest friend. "Who did she talk to?"

"Not talk. Saw. Heard. I only know one of them, a man. Elias Penny is his name. He helped me at my shop one day. Oh, and he's the one who invited me to that Sertoma meeting, which I do plan on joining...if you'll all have me that is. I'm not exactly a local."

"Honey, neither am I, and they let me in. You're a shoe if you've got a few endorsements. He'll probably give you one if you ask him, since he's invited you and all. You're a celebrity and that might be all you need."

She blushed. "I don't want to trade on that."

"Baby, you use what the good Lord gave you. We're women in a man's world. We take what we can get."

From her position in line with Jesse, Faye made mental notes of the other mourners that might bear further scrutiny when she and Chloe could talk privately. Jason and his wife Kasey were there in the line, several people ahead of them. A few people behind Jason and Kasey stood Kent, all alone. Everyone in the village knew he was a married man, but his wife rarely made appearances in town, and when she did, it was usually without him. She was fond of the bakery and Hannah's bread and ventured down to the shop twice a week.

The two men weren't really close together, but Jason kept turning back, eying the other man over and around the mourners lined up between them.

Faye found Chloe still waiting for her in the anteroom when she returned with Jesse. Hattie drifted off to collect Bridget who was still weaving her way about talking to this person and that one.

Jesse asked his wife, "Are you riding with me or with Chloe?"

"I rode over here with Chloe," she answered him, "but I can let her get on along home to get Marco his supper, I guess, if you'll drop me at the store to get my car." She gave Chloe a tight-lipped smile. *We have so much to talk about.*

One of the funeral home workers took pity on the crowd and opened the back emergency door as they gathered themselves to go. They opted to leave that way. It surprised the three of them to find Mel, in uniform, in the parking lot when they made their way out and around the building from the back side.

"What are you doing here?" Jesse asked his daughter.

"I could ask the same of you." She shot a look at her mother and then at Mama Rossi trailing just behind her parents.

"Paying our respects," Faye said.

"And you're staying out of my case?"

"Are you saying she was murdered?"

Jesse guffawed at Faye's return question, then he started coughing.

Mel shot her father a look, but addressed her mother and her mother-in-law behind her. "I said no such thing. I'm simply following up on some police business, so I'm asking you - I won't tell you because that has the opposite effect on the two of you - but I'm asking you to stay out of my case."

CHAPTER 9-SUSPECTS

Faye couldn't wait to get on the phone with Chloe. When they got home, Jesse needed this and that though, so she felt obligated to tend to him first. *Men! When they're sick, it's like the world is ending.*

She fixed him a grilled cheese sandwich and a bowl of her homemade noodle soup for an early dinner and took it to him on a tray so he could eat from his La-Z-Boy.

"Aren't you eating?"

"I'm not hungry just yet," she told him.

He waggled a finger at her. "I know what this is about. You hens want to put your heads together and squawk. Mark my words; you better listen to Melissa and not go sticking your noses into police business."

"We don't have our noses in official police business." *Yet.*

"Make sure you keep it that way."

THIRTY MINUTES later Jesse was snoring loudly in his chair, his dinner only half eaten. She went to the kitchen with his food tray and dispatched his mess quickly away. She was undoing the tie of her waist apron when she heard gravel crunch in the driveway.

She knew it was Chloe. *Hopefully, the dogs figure it out and don't bark.* Jesse would sleep through anything but them making a ruckus. She tossed the apron aside.

They met on the wrap around front porch with Faye giving her friend the 'shh' sign.

Chloe took a seat where she could see the sunset if they were out there long enough, and Faye took one next to her.

"Sweet tea?" Faye asked, jumping back up.

Chloe waved a hand. "No, no. Don't go to any bother. Let's just talk while we can. He could wake up any time."

"He'll be out for a while. You should hear him snoring in there. Only snores when he's feeling out of sorts."

"I wish! Marco snores like a freight train every night."

"Did you eat?"

"Sandwiches. That's all Marco wanted. Anyway, why don't you start and tell me what you saw and then I'll tell you what I saw, and we can make a plan?"

"I don't know," Faye said, doing a slow shake of her head. "Mel seemed pretty hot about us even seeming to be involved, and other than a somewhat heated discussion between Elias Penny and Lucy Sharpe, nothing really caught my attention as very unusual or completely out of place."

"Really? We'll get back to Elias and Lucy in a minute. But honestly, you don't think Blake and Molly having their heads together is suspicious?"

Faye gave that some thought. "It is strange, but that could be anything. He might have been trying to pin her down on a lost package or something."

"She went to him, not him to her."

"True."

"So, we'll put them in the suspicious characters' column. Let's talk about motive. What's Blake's?"

"He's easy," Faye said, shrugging. "He's a crook. Greed, that's his motive for taking the coins…only the most valuable ones."

"And Molly's?"

Faye shook her head. "That one is harder to figure."

"Could she be in a relationship with Blake, or in some sort of criminal cahoots with him? Helping him find things worth stealing?"

"You live a half mile out of the village, and you work in it. What do you think? Have you ever seen them together?"

"Not going in and out of his house, no. But I'm sure they meet up at the post office."

"As does everyone else in the village, with Molly. Besides, there are cameras in there and it's a small place. She'd be awfully hard pressed to take things and get away with it."

"True. But she's not 'taking' them." Chloe said, making air quotes. "She passes along information only."

Faye paused in thought. "Okay, I'll give you that, but remember, if she's not opening packages, she doesn't know what's in them. It would all be speculation on her part based on whatever the markings are. She knew what was going on before anyone else, though. That's suspicious even though the gossip mill around here seems to flood the banks pretty darn fast."

"So, we put Molly in a maybe category. Where does that leave Blake?"

"Still a crook," Faye said.

"So, we put him firmly in the suspect category." It wasn't a question.

Faye nodded.

"Who else are we calling a suspect for sure?"

"Hattie."

Her quick answer seemed to surprise Chloe. "What? Why? You really don't like her, do you?"

Faye let the last question slide, ticking her reasons for suspecting the young woman off her fingers. "She lost her job and her major source of income. She's trying to start a business. You know yourself how much money that takes. She's starting from scratch. And she's got a nose in everyone's business, especially surrounding this whole affair."

"Her aunt brought her into it," Chloe reminded her.

"Right, and that brings me to means. She lives with Bridget, so she'd have access there. She knows Selma, though I'll admit that the connection is murky, but she certainly could have picked up on a coin conversation between her aunt and Selma."

"That doesn't explain Delores."

"She had plenty of opportunity to learn about Delores if you think about it. Bridgett could have talked about her coin collecting if they did that sort of thing together. Also, she's setting up shop right next door to Delores' home in a place she rented from the Chappells. She probably knew Delores was back there, staying in her house when no one else did, probably not even realizing how odd that would be since she should have been in prison."

Chloe shook her head slowly. "I hear all of that, but my gut says no. Not Hattie. Remember that it was Selma that told us she did things with coins with Delores, not Bridgett."

"But Hattie was standing right there when Selma told us that and that was before they found Delores." Faye said, throwing her hands up. "What's your attachment to her? She's a celebrity? The entire aura thing?"

Chloe sighed. "No attachment. How about this? For the sake of peace, let's put her in the maybe column and we'll look into it. I think we have some better suspects."

"Suit yourself," Faye said. "I say she's a suspect and we treat her like one if we're going to do this."

"Who else should we look at?" Chloe asked, steering the topic away from Hattie.

Faye was quick again. "I know I said I saw nothing else unusual, but thinking it over now, I'm thinking about Kent Gross and Jason Meyer. They were both there tonight and shooting each other odd looks."

Chloe said, "I believe they're in cahoots about something, but they don't strike me as coin thieves. Gross is a wealthy man."

"Yes, but there was no reason on earth for him to be there today," Faye said. "There's no way he knew her except possibly in passing. He's only been around here a few years. He pushed his way into the Sertoma presidency, against my better judgment. That's always gone to long-time residents with a lot of community respect. He has none of that."

"Good point. Jason has lived here for years, though, right? He would have known her pretty well, most likely."

"He grew up nearby and Kasey grew up in the village, so yes. His thing is, he always needs money. That pizza shop is in a century old building like most of the rest of the village. It's a money pit. Knowing the value of those coins, he could have taken them to pawn or sell to a collector."

"From all three women? How would he have known about all of them?" Chloe answered her own question at the same time Faye answered, "Blake."

Chloe said, "Blake must be the tie in all of this—"

Nodding along, Faye put in, "Yes, Blake. He's in cahoots with Kent all the time. Jason is in cahoots with Kent now over something. What if whatever Kent and Jason are cooking up required Jason to have a bigger bankroll and Kent pointed Blake in his direction to help him out—"

"Or Blake saw a chance to get a bigger stake for himself?"

Chloe finished. "Let's move Kent to the middle, but put Jason in the suspect column. And we still haven't talked about Elias. You said he and Lucy Sharpe were arguing?"

"I don't know that I'd call it outright arguing. Lucy seemed... perturbed. It sounded like she expected something from Elias that he didn't follow through on."

"Coin grading?"

"Again, I don't know," Faye said as she splayed out a hand toward her friend. "I was late to listen in on all of that, if they even said what they were going on about. It all just raises suspicion for me because he told us he's done grading for her in the past and he might know about all the collectors in the village too, especially if any of them bought anything from Lucy and, say maybe, he was around to see it."

"What would his motive be?"

"Greed as well?" Faye tossed up a hand again. "He knows as much as any of the collectors what those coins would be worth. His mother just died after being laid up in a nursing home. Care isn't cheap and neither are funerals, even if they just did a cremation or a burial."

"Hmm. That gives us Blake, Jason, and Elias to look at as primary suspects. Hattie and Molly are secondary suspects."

"And Kent," Faye reminded her.

"Yes. Kent on the possibilities list. Anyone else?"

"Don't you think that's more than enough?" She didn't wait for an answer. "Besides, one of them is involved in this somehow."

"What do we want to do now?" Chloe asked.

"We poke around... discreetly. I don't need Jesse or my daughter knowing what we're doing."

"We need to watch Blake."

"Watch? There's no way we can easily do that. We've learned that the hard way. He'd be onto us, no matter what. We just need to figure out a way to talk to him...publicly, of course, and find out what we want to know."

"Or we get Dana involved and she finds out what Mel knows for us," Chloe offered.

"Too risky. Mel will see right through that. I'll just have to figure something out."

"I can poke around about Jason, see what he might be up to. I don't feel odd going into the pizza shop and Kasey comes into the store a lot. She's a talker, more so than he is."

"Yeah, we'll get more talking to her than we will spying on him," Faye agreed. "What about Elias? We can't really go back to his house and snoop around."

"I know just the thing," Chloe said, wagging a finger much as Jesse had an hour or so before. "We can talk to Lucy Sharpe after church tomorrow. She's a talker too. Bet we can get out of her what the problem with Elias was, see if there's anything related to this...to our case. He may do a lot more grading than he's letting on."

Faye gave a brief nod. "That actually sounds reasonable. The only thing Mel could take issue with in all of it is if she catches me talking to Blake."

"Make it obvious," Chloe instructed. "When you do it, do it right out in the open, like you said. It's the safest way, anyway. Have anything in mind?"

"He's not going anywhere. I'll have to think about it some. In the meantime, let's keep Hattie out of all of it. I won't go chasing after her if you don't read her into all of this. Deal?"

"Deal."

"We're forgetting someone," Faye said.

"Two people. There's still Molly and Kent. Let's split them. You take Molly, since she's easy to find and loves to gossip, since you've already got Blake the hard case. I'll figure out how to work on Kent, but I'm going to put him last on my list. I think Jason is more key to solving this than he is."

The screen door swung open. "What's going on out here?" Jesse asked.

Faye was quick with a response. "We're just chatting and enjoying the sunset. You fell asleep practically in your soup bowl. I hope you're feeling better."

CHAPTER 10–CHURCH LADIES

Sunday, September 25th

Chloe slid up next to Lucy Sharpe where she stood near the coffee urn stirring creamer into her foam cup of steaming brew. "Don't mind me," she began. "I just need a little sugar with my caffeine today."

Lucy gave her a raised eyebrow look. "You don't normally take it with sugar?"

"Well, a little," Chloe backtracked. "I just need more today." As Lucy moved away, she followed. "It's been a crazy few days, hasn't it?"

Lucy gave a prim nod. "That it has." She took a cookie from Hannah, the only professional baker in the village, who was doling them out at a table next to the urn and thanked her.

Chloe pointed at the table where Faye sat. "Would you like to join us?"

"Oh." Lucy looked stricken. "I usually sit with Selma and Bridget and the other...older, um, members of the congregation."

The old biddies and busybodies. Chloe tried another tack.

"That's okay then. We just had something we wanted to chat with you about, but I guess it's not so important it can't wait until tomorrow... oh wait. No, I can't come and see you tomorrow. Maybe Tuesday then. Wait. That's not good either. Oh, dear."

Lucy bit. "Maybe just for a minute."

Chloe shot Faye a triumphant grin from behind Lucy as she followed her over to their table.

Faye had chosen their seats wisely. She put herself at the far end of a ten-foot folding table well out of the traffic pattern to the coffee and refreshment tables. Chloe figured they had some time before anyone, but the pastor would bother to venture their way to make small talk. She only needed a couple of minutes.

Lucy wasn't about wasting time herself. She jumped right in with, "What did you want to talk about?"

Faye jerked backward in her folding chair a little, but Chloe began with the story she'd already used once. "A family member of mine, my daughter-in-law, Shannon," *whom you'll never meet*, "has come into a small estate on the passing of a family member of hers."

Lucy tilted her head and gave her a strange look. "Oh. Well, certainly my condolences on her loss, but how does that involve me?"

"It was a much older relative," Chloe said. "He had a lot of antiques and collectibles in his home." She waved a hand dismissively. "Shannon is dealing with most of it, but he collected coins and she doesn't know what to do with those."

"I'm not a coin dealer, per se, you see. And I can't value them for you... er, for her."

"We know," Faye said. "We've already talked to Elias Penny about getting them valued."

Lucy pulled a face, but she masked it quickly.

Chloe jumped back in. "When he explained things to us, we realized some coins have already been graded and slabbed.

Shannon has no interest in keeping those. Some of his other collectibles, yes. Memories, you see, but not the coins. Elias said you might be interested in taking the ones that already have values established on them in on consignment?" She fixed Lucy with what she hoped was a hopeful look.

"Elias recommended that?"

Faye nodded. "Yes. He said he's graded some coins for you in the past that you received into your shop."

"He has." Her tone was firm, bordering on anger.

"Is something wrong?" Faye asked gently.

"No, nothing." The tear forming in her right eye told a different story.

Chloe threw an arm around the other woman's shoulders. "We're so sorry. We didn't mean to upset you."

"Not at all," Faye added.

Lucy pulled a white handkerchief embroidered with a single rose in one corner out of her pocketbook and dabbed at one eye. "I apologize for getting emotional. It's not your fault."

"Something we can help with?" Chloe asked.

The older woman dabbed at her other eye as she shook her head slowly. "It's me. I had an argument with Elias just yesterday at the funeral parlor of all places. He insists he returned a full set of coins to me that were part of a fairly extensive collection I took in. I was sure he didn't. Not all of them."

Chloe shot Faye a look.

"I can't find a few of the coins," Lucy continued. "I paid the seller for them outright, based on what I know myself and on what I've learned from Elias over the years. The missing coins are some of the most valuable ones in the collection. I'd have been sure to make my money back on the whole purchase from just those."

Faye reached out to her too, taking hold of her hand. "Could they have been taken from your shop before or after you took them to Elias?"

Lucy sniffled. "I don't think so, but maybe. I...I just put everything like that into a case in the back until I have a place to display it. My great niece comes down on her school breaks from college and puts some stuff on that Internet for me. A lot of the coins go on there, so I put them away until she can take the pictures and put them on."

Chloe did her best to mask her curiosity and appear as being supportive. "So, mostly, they're not being sold to locals and people passing through?"

A small smile crossed Lucy's lips. "As if people just 'pass through' Morelville."

"True," Faye admitted. "We're not on the way to anywhere, here."

"Lying in church," Faye said as she shook a finger at Chloe from the passenger seat of Chloe's car. "We're both going to pay for that."

"It was for a good cause, you know. We learned some new things for our case."

"Our case? Listen to you. Melissa will have our heads!"

"We learned nothing we need to go running to Mel with," Chloe said, "so we're safe there." *For a minute, anyway.* "We know now that we need to move Elias up as a full suspect."

"Why? We don't even know if they were Carson City coins," Faye said. "I mean, what are the odds of even more of those coming into this tiny village? It would seem like those are so valuable because they're so rare."

"What are the odds a coin grader lives here, or a millionaire land developer, or a retired big-city police lieutenant," she said, referring to her own husband Marco, "or—"

"Point taken," Faye said. "So, now what do we do?"

Family Fun Day
The Crane Family Farm
Morelville, Ohio

Kris slid up next to Mel as she worked out in the horse pasture, trying to hold two gate panels up and connect them together.

"Good. Glad you're here," her twin said, when she spotted her. "Dad wants a round pen out here for Beth to use when she works the horses. I could use a hand."

Kris looked around. "Where are Dad and Cole?"

"They went down to the barn for more connecting rods. They never came back."

Kris glanced at the pile of rods laying at Mel's feet. "Looks like you've got plenty." She held the second steel gate up while Mel slid the first one closer and lined their hinges up then dropped rods into the top and bottom latches.

"Two down, ten or twelve to go," she said.

"Listen, Mel," Kris said as she spread the two gates out a little further while her sister walked back to fetch another one from the stack leaning against the pasture fence, "I'm actually glad it's just you and me right now. I wanted to talk to you about Beth."

Mel glanced sideways at her sister. "What about her?"

"She had one of her visions Tuesday night."

Mel averted her face and stared at her feet.

Kris knew her twin was already shutting her off. "Listen. She saw Delores dead before it even happened. Ask Lance. He'll tell you the same thing. He got home earlier than we expected. He was the first one in her room in the middle of the night when she called out. No one found Delores until Wednesday."

Mel snugged the third gate up to the second one and stooped

to pick up two more connecting rods. "So, what is it you want me to do?"

"Well, first off, I'm asking everyone not to talk about it. Beth was at school when Delores was found. She doesn't need to hear about it. It'll just freak her out."

"It happened what? Four days ago, now? If she doesn't already know, especially since there's been a funeral, she's going to find out, you know?" Mel said to her twin. "There's no way to keep it from her. Besides, it's looking like she had a heart attack and died from natural causes. There's nothing concerning there."

Kris encountered the same sort of push back inside the farmhouse later when they all were preparing for supper.

Chloe, who was over visiting with Faye and Jesse, was the first one to point out, "You can't keep anything quiet; not in this town," she said. "I learned that pretty fast." She shot a glance at Faye. Her friend looked away and pretended to concentrate on breaking up greens for the dinner salad.

"What did she see?" Chloe turned back to Kris and asked her instead.

"From the sounds of it, she saw exactly what happened or, at least, the aftermath of what happened."

Jesse, as skeptical as his wife Faye was about their granddaughter's visions, interrupted. "You don't suppose she saw Delores come back, do ya? And then maybe she kind of played out a brief scene out in her head because she saw her?"

Kris answered, "Unfortunately, there's no way to know that without talking to her about it. I don't want to stir that up again. She was terrified the other night."

From her position at the kitchen table, slicing tomatoes, Mel sighed. "Look, all of you; this is a lot of doing about nothing. Delores developed a heart condition while she was in prison...or it showed up then, anyway. She was 82, for Pete's sake! Tennessee considered her a low-risk prisoner from a state standpoint, so they released her to a long-term care facility. No one knows for sure why she was at her house and not there. If they do, they're not saying. Maybe her death was a forgone conclusion and the family brought her home to live out her last days. Maybe Hospice was involved. Who knows, but that's the only mystery here and I can run that down really quick."

Faye couldn't contain herself any longer. "The rumor mill is saying the police found her surrounded by a mess; her coin collection spread around everywhere," she said, as she looked pointedly at her daughter. "Is that true, Melissa?"

Mel visibly bristled at her mother using her full name. She started to nod, seemed to stop herself and gave a half shrugged, instead. "I wouldn't call it a mess. Maybe organized chaos is a better term. She had it piled all around; kind of like she was sorting through her things. For all we know, she was doing a final accounting... what to pass on to whom sort of thing."

Chloe raised her eyebrows at Faye and then asked her own question. "Did anyone bring anything up to you about her coins, Mel?"

The younger woman shook her head. "No. Should they have? Have you heard something?"

"No, no...just asking. So, they weren't...I don't know, tossed around down there, then?"

"Tossed? No. They were scattered, but it didn't strike me as an actual mess or that they'd been tossed in a search for something or anything like that. There was a lot of stuff; stuff I never knew she had..." she trailed off, thinking.

Faye was skeptical. "Mel, think. Remember how orderly Delores always was about her things? Anyone who went there to use her notary services could see that she had a place for everything and everything in its place. Why, look at what an easy time you had finding all the evidence that sent her up the river in the first place, poor old woman."

Mel's eyes narrowed. She looked back and forth between Chloe and Faye and shook a finger at them. "That woman died of natural causes brought on by old age. Don't you two go thinking there's some sort of case here for you to stick your noses into. There was no crime."

"Us?" Chloe said, her best look of innocence plastered on her face. "Why, we wouldn't dream of it."

"Trust me; we've learned our lesson," Fayed added, as she nodded along with the whole charade.

Jesse guffawed loudly.

"Why don't you take me down to the barn and show me the horses?" Chloe asked Beth after dinner.

"Really? You really want to see them?"

"Absolutely. My granddaughter has been agitating us to get her a horse she can ride, now that we live out in the country, as she likes to remind us every chance she gets."

"Now Mama, we're not getting her a horse," Marco called out from his chair on the porch.

Chloe flipped a hand in his direction, but she didn't bother to look at him.

"I'm serious Chloe! She lives in Pittsburgh, for cripe's sake! Who's going to end up taking care of it? Us, that's who!"

Beth smiled. "You don't have to get her one, Mr. Rossi. She can come out here and ride mine...ours. I'll teach her."

Smiling, "Lead on," Chloe said to the teenager. "Let's go look at what's got you all excited."

"We've had horses for a while now. I've been riding since I was pretty little. This is the first year Grandpa said he'd let me show one at the fair. He sort of gave in," she confided. "I kept asking him to let me show a steer like Cole does or to do horses along with my calf."

Faye smiled at the light in Beth's eyes as she spoke. She could feel her excitement. As they walked the wide path to the barn, the girl babbled on about horses and riding the entire way.

In the barn, Beth stopped in a front stall, lifted a tarp, and pulled a few flakes of hay off of a bale. Handing one to Chloe, she said, "We'll get them interested in us with these. They've been out in the pasture all day, but they'll always come to the front of the stall for hay."

At the next stall, Beth dropped one of her flakes into the feed bucket hanging on the inside of the half door. The horse came right to it.

Chloe laughed. "You know them well."

"This one is Chet," the girl said. "He's grandpa's horse."

"Really? Jesse rides?"

"Well, yeah. That's how come we have horses out here at all."

"I've never seen him on a horse."

"He uses the UTV a lot now...says riding's hard on his back, but in the summer, when it's hot and his back doesn't bother him so much, he'll ride, especially when he's out checking the fence. You'll see."

"Chet is pretty gentle. Cole rides him sometimes if Grandpa is in the mood to let him." She moved two stalls down and Chloe followed. The mare in the stall was already standing at her gate. "Drop your flake in her bucket," the teen said. "This is old Helen. She's the horse that would be good for Shannon to learn on. She might not know what to do, but Helen does."

"Is this the one you ride?" Chloe asked, as she patted the horse's neck, mimicking Beth's movements on the other side.

"No. She was Grandma's horse, but she never rides her anymore. Mom and Aunt Mel take her out sometimes and visitors that want to ride. Mine is the chestnut filly over there. She's only two years old and she's the one Mom is helping me train to show." She pointed behind them, across the aisle, then turned from Helen and walked across to the stall.

"And what's her name?" Chloe asked her from a few feet behind her.

"We got her at a horse auction. She had a stupid name, I thought...Rosie. I've been calling her Jenna. Grandpa doesn't like that name though, so I don't know."

"Really? Well, I think Jenna suits her," Chloe said as she watched the horse dance a bit when it saw the flake of hay Beth reached over the gate with.

Beth broke some off and fed it to the filly by hand, then put the rest in the bucket.

Chloe thought about how best to broach the subject she really wanted to talk about. She decided being direct was best. "Beth, Shannon really wants a horse, and she wants to learn to ride, but that's not really why I brought you down here."

The teenager looked over at her but said nothing, waiting and listening.

"I know you overheard most of the conversation we were having in the kitchen before dinner."

Beth's eyes darted away, back to Jenna. The color drained from her face.

"It's okay," Chloe told her. "I sensed you were just around the corner. You probably sensed that the sort of conversation we were having was coming, didn't you?"

Beth's eyes grew wide. "Ha...how did you know?"

"Because I know you see other things too, especially in your dreams."

"You believe me?"

Chloe nodded. "Of course. I have visions too. I've had them all my life."

"Really?"

"Mine are mostly good things, but sometimes, they're a little scary."

Beth reached out to the still eating Jenna and stroked her mane. "All of mine seem scary." She took in a deep breath and let it out in a huff. Her face regained some of its color.

"Do you want to talk about this latest one...or any of your visions, for that matter? It might help."

"My Great Grandma called them premonitions."

Chloe smiled and gave the girl a quick hug as she whispered, "So did mine."

"They really found that woman there? She was dead?"

"Yes, baby. They found her."

The girl shuddered.

Faye pulled her into a hug again, a little tighter that time.

CHAPTER 11–CLUING IN THE SHERIFF

Monday, September 26th
Muskingum County Sheriff's Department
Zanesville, Ohio

"I'm here to see Mel," Chloe told Holly, the Sergeant who served as Mel's assistant.

"Give me just a minute, Mama Rossi," Holly asked. "Let me see what she's got herself into. Please," she held out a hand, "have a seat. It might be a few minutes." With that, she left the outer area and went down the little hallway to Mel's office.

As she tapped on Mel's door, she thought to herself, "*This can't be good*."

"Yeah?" Mel called out.

Holly opened the door that was usually always open. "Bad time, Sheriff?"

"I'm just trying to get a handle on these reports and the spreadsheets I have to do. It's crazy the stuff the state wants. This is why I didn't really want to be the Sheriff and it's probably why I won't run for re-election. Anyway, I could use a break right about now. What do you need?"

Holly shifted her face away as she rolled her eyes at Mel, saying she wouldn't run again and then looked back at her friend turned boss. "I don't know if this will give you the sort of break you're looking for. Your mother-in-law is here asking for you."

Mel gave Holly a funny look. "Why? I just saw her yesterday. She didn't say anything to me then."

"Sorry. She didn't say."

"She didn't say, or you didn't ask?" Mel ribbed her.

"Both."

Mel blew out a breath. "Send her back. Anything that she wants to talk about can't be as bad as working on these spreadsheets."

"Shouldn't you be opening the store, Mama Rossi?"

"Your mom is helping Marco this morning. She looked in on Hannah first, but that girl's got that bakery of hers well under control."

Chloe looked at Mel's desk, noting the scattered paperwork. "I can see you're busy," she began, not wasting any time. "I just want to tell you, you're making a big mistake not looking more into Delores Chappell's death."

"Delores had a heart attack. The coroner confirmed it. I didn't say that yesterday, and I really shouldn't have told you now."

Chloe wasn't swayed. "Did the coroner know what caused it?"

"Like I said yesterday, she was over 80. Could have been natural causes. Could have been scared by a mouse."

"We both know better than that."

Mel steepled her hands over her paperwork. "Oh? Why is that? And please, no more talk about premonitions."

"Agreed. Now, promise me what I'm about to tell you won't

leave this room?"

Mel held out a hand. "Mama Rossi, you know I can't do that. If there's a crime involved…"

Chloe interrupted her daughter-in-law. "Just hear me out. I've been sworn to secrecy, but I think this thing has grown larger than the original problem."

"What problem?"

Chloe leaned in a little and began, "Selma Morrison came into the store the other day. It seems she has some coins missing; some *very* valuable coins. And it's not just her. Bridget Novak is missing coins, too."

"Neither of them has reported a theft to this department that I'm aware of," Mel said.

"I know. That's the part they…well, at least Selma, wanted kept secret. She doesn't want word to get out that she has a highly valuable coin collection in her home."

"Somebody knows," Mel pointed out, before asking a question of her own. "And now they think this is all tied together with Delores, somehow? We haven't let out any information about her…the circumstances of her…well, her coins, other than what we talked about yesterday. I've told my family far more than I should have done already."

So, coins surrounded her when she was found. "Well…I haven't exactly talked to them yet. You wanted me and Faye to stay out of it, remember?"

Mel restrained herself from visibly reacting to the comment. "True. So, it's you two who think it's tied together? On what grounds?"

"Nothing concrete, you understand." Her conversation with Beth flashed through her mind. "It's just that Blake Wagner's name came up in our conversation with Selma. He's one of the few that both knew she had coins and who knows where she lives. He's…he's just such an unsavory character, Mel. I could see him breaking into Delores's place, thinking it was empty and scaring her into a heart attack, in her fragile state." Chloe looked right through Mel as she thought to herself, '*And your niece told me she saw a man, all dressed in black, in her vision.*'

"You haven't gone and poked at Wagner, have you?"

Chloe shook her head. "No. Not at all. I don't want to be anywhere near him. Why, we saw him at the funeral with dozens of people around and we didn't go near him then. I'll leave that to you. I just thought you should know. So does your mother."

Mel rubbed her face with her hands. "All right then. I'll look into it."

"Discreetly?"

"Yes, discreetly."

"Promise?"

Mel shook her head. "Do you promise to stay out of it from here on?"

Chloe turned to leave.

Mel called after her, "Mama Rossi, promise me!"

The older woman looked back over her shoulder. "All I can say is, I'll do my best."

Tuesday Morning, September 27th
Morelville, Ohio

Mel stood on Selma Morrison's little side porch, her hat in her hand. She knocked on the frame of the screen door softly. Lights were on in the back of the house, but she couldn't see anyone moving about inside. She didn't want to wake Selma if she wasn't up.

The older woman came to the door in a dressing gown. "Is there something wrong, Melissa?" she asked when she opened it, concern showing in her features.

"I'm sorry for stopping by so early. I saw your lights on and thought this might be the best time to talk with you...discreetly."

Sighing, Selma stepped aside and waved Mel in. "Let's go back to the kitchen. I just put the coffee on."

"That's kind of you, but none for me, thanks."

Mel rubbed the back of her neck with her free hand. "Given your reaction just now, I imagine you know why I'm here?"

Selma nodded as she stepped over to the counter beside the sink, picked up a mug and poured herself her first cup of coffee for the day. "There are no secrets in Morelville. I ought to know that by now. I suppose it's just as well. Delores is dead, God rest her soul, and I'm sure it's related to my...issue."

Turning, she waved a hand at the scrubbed wood table. "Please sit."

Mel did as she was told.

"What makes you think Delores's death is related to your missing coins?"

"Please Melissa; the only thing faster than lightning around here is the rumor mill. Everyone is talking about how she was killed, surrounded by a mess of her...things."

"She wasn't killed," Mel said. "She had a heart attack." She didn't bother to argue the other point. Instead, she said, "I'm here about *your* missing coins. There may or may not be any connection to anything to do with Delores. I'm just trying to get some sort of picture of what I might be dealing with. Can you tell me about what you've had taken?"

Selma placed her steaming mug down carefully and then took a seat opposite Mel. As she stirred sugar and then cream into the cup, she gave Mel a quick overview of the coins now absent from her collection. "I have a full inventory of everything I have...or, should I say, that I had. I can give you a list of what's gone missing."

"That's helpful," Mel said. "Any chance you have photos of the coins?"

Selma shook her head. "Never thought I'd need them. Coins don't photograph well anyway unless you have all the right equipment. Delores mail ordered...used to mail order stuff. You never know what you're getting with that. I always went to auctions so I could see the stuff I wanted firsthand."

"I'll need your list then," Mel told her, "And, I'm going to have to have you do a sworn statement."

Selma let out a long sigh.

"Look at the bright side," Mel told her. "I'll do a report. You can take that and file an insurance claim and then, when that pays, you can buy more coins."

The older woman smiled. "That's true, but that money is already spoken for. I'm sure it will thrill your mom and Chloe Rossi when the insurance company pays the claim and I hand that check over."

Mel raised a hand in the air to stop Selma from saying anymore. "I don't even want to know."

Mel took a quick look around Delores Chappell's home as her patrol sergeant and one of her detectives, Janet Mason, went about dusting it for fingerprints. Seeing all that was there, it did not convince her, her long-time neighbor hadn't been startled into her death over her coins.

"There's a lot of stuff laying everywhere, Sheriff," Janet said to her when she made her way into the kitchen. "Do we do anything with these coins?" She waved a hand at a wood display box and the coins arrayed around it on a rolling cart next to the stove.

Mel tapped a finger against her chin, thinking for a moment.

She told her, "Dust the flat surfaces and the display boxes but not the coins. She may have spread these all out like this or someone else that didn't know where something was may have emptied each box looking for specific coins." She glanced around the kitchen where every available surface was covered with similar display boxes and the coins they housed. They also covered the small living room.

"Stick mostly to the kitchen. More surfaces in here, and it is where we found her, after all. The family wants to get in here and clean this up, now that they have laid her to rest. No sense in us coating absolutely everything with our powder and making their job three, maybe four times as hard."

CHAPTER 12–SERTOMA MEETING

7:05 PM, Tuesday Evening
Sertoma Service Club Meeting
Morelville Community Center
Morelville, Ohio

"The Chair recognizes Elias Penny." Kent Gross said, as he picked up his gavel and smacked it down on the sounding block.

Chloe hunched her shoulders toward her ears when he did it. She whispered to Marco, as they both watched Elias get to his feet, "We're going to rue the day we ever elected him President, if he keeps that up every time he opens his mouth."

Marco gave his wife's leg a quick pat, but he kept his eyes on Elias.

Elias stood, looked around the room, then turned toward Hattie and smiled before beginning with, "Everyone, before we get started this evening, I asked Kent if I could say a few words."

Mildred remained seated beside him, her hands folded in front of her on the table. She glanced up at him as he began, but then trained her eyes on her hands.

"First, I want to say thank you to those of you who reached

out while we were away tending to the needs of my mother before she passed. Your kind words and offers of help were very much appreciated."

There were murmurs around the room. Chloe leaned to her right toward Faye and whispered, "He didn't mention that when we talked to him last week. Did you know?"

Faye glanced across her friend at Marco, who was eying them both and simply shook her head.

Elias raised a hand. "That's not all. We also have a guest, and hopefully a future member of our little group here with us tonight. If you didn't get here in time to meet her before we got started, I'd like to introduce Miss Hattie Novak. Some of you probably recognize her," he went on, as he turned away from Hattie's shaking head, "as the actress Althea Dwyer. She...she played the role of Bree Crunk, from the uh, television show, uh, The Crestview Crunks." He glanced at Chloe and then away as he spoke about Hattie's television work.

All eyes in the room focused on Hattie except for Chloe's. She continued to watch Elias. *He sure seems to know all about her for a man that claims not to watch much TV,* she thought.

"Hattie is opening a shop in the village," Elias added. "I'm hoping we can convince her to join us."

Hattie blushed as applause sounded from around the room.

Kent banged his gavel again, driving everyone to silence. "Welcome Miss Novak. Please see me after the meeting. Now, for our first order of new business..."

Faye Crane stood from her position, seated next to Kent. "Point of order."

Heads nodded around the room.

The developer sucked in a breath. "Yes, Mrs. Crane?"

"Two things. First, welcome Miss Novak. If you think you'd like to become a member of our group, you'll need to see me after the meeting for a membership application." Faye turned slightly toward Kent as she went on, "Though I'm sure Mr. Gross would like to speak with you first. And, second, Mr. Gross, we try to follow the normal order of business, as laid out in Robert's Rules of Order, unless something is pressing. Typically, we cover my Secretary's report, the Treasurer's report, committee reports and then old business, before we get to new business." She gave him a smug little smile and sat back down.

"She's correct," Elias called out. "I know it's your first go-around up there at the podium. I've got an extra copy of the book back at the house, if you need one."

Chloe whispered to Marco, "He's still feeling burned by Kent beating him for President and now slighting him...him and Hattie. Can you tell?"

Marco had the good grace not to answer.

"Now, can we talk about new business?" Kent asked as he resumed the podium and looked toward Faye, forty-five minutes later.

She nodded in his direction as laughter rose in the room.

The chair picked up his gavel and pointed it at Jason Meyer. "Mr. Meyer, you have the floor." He took his chair then, grinning as he sat.

Chloe eyed Jason suspiciously. *He rarely comes to the meetings, so he must want something.*

Jason didn't bother to stand. He sketched a wave at the group as he said, "Hi everybody. Sorry, I...me and Kasey, haven't been here much lately. We've been busy with the business and all."

He swallowed hard and looked around. "It's hard for me to ask for help, but I'm needing some, and that's what I want to talk to you all about."

Chloe leaned forward in her chair, vindicated for the moment, but wondering just what it was he was about to ask.

"Faye and Mrs. Rossi over there," he said, "have been

heading up a project to do some renovations on that old church I own. Unfortunately, I...we've had to put so much money into the business, we haven't been able to help much at all with money and fund-raising."

You haven't put dime one in, Chloe thought.

"Before their major renovations start in the spring, we need to look at the situation with the land."

"We, Jason?" Craig Stroud asked.

Jason nodded. "This group. I know, I know," he waved a hand, "the township owns the actual property, minus the building. See, that's not an ideal situation, if we want to make the building functional for...for...well, you know."

Marco jumped in before Chloe could. "Functional for what? It's just supposed to be a chapel, right?"

"Well, yeah, but it's going to need a new, bigger water well. We need to upgrade the bathrooms and plumb them into the sewage they put in a few years ago, after the church had been shuttered for a while, and... Anyway, what I'm proposing is that the Sertoma group buy the land off of the township."

Several people started talking at once.

Kent banged the gavel down four times, hard. "The chair has recognized no other speakers."

Chloe rose and waited until Kent recognized her. "This," she said as she looked back and forth between Jason and Kent, "is the first I'm hearing of this. It's just a small church we want to preserve and possibly use as chapel, from time to time. A tiny church. There's no need for any of those things and, even if there were, the township would let us dig a well and so forth. I don't see the need for us to spend money we don't have for things we don't need."

"Hear, hear!" Elias called out. "I second that sentiment." Beside him, his wife Mildred sat back in her chair, arms crossed, and lips pursed. She stared at Kent, eyes unwavering.

"Let's not be too hasty," Kent said. "Mr. Meyer presented us with a proposal. It deserves proper consideration." He waited patiently for once, while people talked among themselves for a minute and then gaveled them quiet again. "I propose a committee to look into the matter."

"Is the chair making a motion?" Elias called out. Mildred shook her head.

Kent sucked in a breath. "I move a special committee be appointed to look into the purchase of the land the old Baptist church sits on and that we table further discussion until they report back at our next meeting."

"Second!" Jason called out.

"Show of hands, all in favor?" He counted eight raised hands. "Opposed, same sign."

Chloe, Marco, Faye, and Elias raised their hands.

"Motion carried."

"Point of order!" Faye called out as she jumped to her feet. "There are at least ten people in here who didn't vote at all."

Kent shrugged. "They abstained. It's a fair ruling."

Chloe whispered to Marco, "Oh, so now he's an expert on the rules of order."

Marco got to his feet. "I volunteer to be on the investigative committee." Faye and Elias followed suit.

Kent wasn't having it. "I think two people are enough. The Chair appoints Marco Rossi and," he looked at Jason and then thought better of it, "Craig."

Craig Stroud got to his feet. "While I'm not opposed to serving on the committee, I have to say I feel like this group is being railroaded into something blindly here." He paused and glanced about, taking in several nodding heads. "The township has shown no inclination to sell that land in the past."

"It serves them no purpose," Jason interjected, before being shushed by Elias.

"Second," Craig went on, "At what cost to Sertoma to acquire it, and for what advantage? We can't do anything with that land. Why not just offer to help fundraise for the building restoration?"

Tongues started wagging for a third time. As Kent raised his gavel, Jason stood up. Rather than rap the gavel on the sounding block, he pointed it toward his friend. "Mr. Meyer."

Mildred Penny stood and spoke before Jason could. "I don't know what Jason's angle is." Elias tried to take her hand and pull her back down, but she wasn't having it. "No offense to Mr. Rossi over there; I'm sure he's more than qualified to serve, but I believe we need someone else on that committee, or at least a third person. Someone local with long-standing ties to this community. Someone who gets what that church means and what that property means."

Jason, who never took his seat, threw up his hands. "What the property means? It's a lousy acre of land!"

Mildred's eyes bored into him. "Then why is it so important we purchase it from the township? They've had no quibble with the restoration so far!"

Elias finally got her to resume her seat. As she situated herself, he whispered, "You can't do that without being recognized. You were out of order."

"Mr. Meyer? A three-person committee?" Kent asked.

"Whatever. I'm...I'm done with it."

"I'll be on your committee," a voice called out from the back of the room. All eyes turned toward Faye's husband, Jesse Crane. "Sorry to be late, but no matter." He covered his mouth and coughed. "I'll just stay back here because I think I've come down with a little something, but as far as the question at hand, I think I've heard as much as I needed to hear."

CHAPTER 13–MISSING MAN

Mel strode into the briefing room and shook her head at her lieutenant, Lomas Gates, standing at the lectern, giving the patrol notes to the oncoming shift.

"Sheriff?" he asked, as he sidestepped to give her room to take his place.

"Sorry to interrupt folks," she said, addressing the room full of deputies. "A quiet day in the county just got crazy. We have a missing persons report that's time sensitive. We need to find this fellow before dark. I've already called mounted search and rescue and they're mobilizing."

"What do we have?" Gates asked.

"We've already had reports about ginseng poachers being out there down around Blue Rock and in my neck of the woods, Morelville. Had them for the last few weeks, at least. Lotta sightings; a lot of missing, known product on private property; nobody caught. Well, we don't think anyone's been caught.

Some of our kindred out there might shoot first and ask no questions."

Heads nodded around the room, but no one smiled. They knew she wasn't just talking.

"It seems two men out of Columbus have been working together, mapping out their scouting location each evening, getting dropped off in the morning right before first light at one edge of what they plotted. They get picked up at the far edge of their plot area in the early afternoon. They get their haul back to Columbus to cash in before their buyer closes up shop."

"Let me guess," Lomas said, "One of them didn't make the pick up point?"

"Last night, right. Name's Steve Hanford."

"Last night?" Joe Treadway asked from his position at a writing desk in the first row, near the door. "And now it's time sensitive? He ain't come in since yesterday, so he's probably in a trap somewhere or worse. Coyote. Bear, maybe."

Mel dipped her head her Sergeant's way in acknowledgment. "I called for search as soon as I got the report, about an hour ago, but that's not the half of it. Their hunting ground yesterday was primarily on my aunt and uncle's property. The Lafferty's. About forty acres of their deep woods and then another twelve or fifteen acres that belong to some Amish that own land that's next to theirs." Mel swallowed. She knew her uncle Brian was a good man, but she also knew he didn't take kindly to trespassers or poachers. His land was heavily posted with warnings. He was as likely as anyone in that area to shoot on sight.

"Yeah," she went on, "I guess the other guy, a Marc Salyers, and their driver waited around as long as they could hang around out there yesterday without drawing a lot of suspicion. Tried calling Hanford's cell. No service out there."

"Salyers says they knew they were running out of season and butting up against bow hunting. They picked a bigger area on purpose and split up; something they rarely do. Salyers showed up at the pickup point with about ten minutes to spare. Said Hanford had a compass and knew how to use it, but when he didn't come out of the woods after more than an hour, they left."

"Who's the driver?" Gates asked.

Mel pointed an index finger at him. "Always on it, Lomas. Unfortunately, we don't know. We're working on him for that, but he's not willing to give anyone else up. Right now, we're not treating him like a suspect in anything, so he hasn't lawyered up, but he's scared."

You had to drive through Morelville to get to her aunt and uncle's place. There wasn't any way to avoid it. As luck would have it, Mel's mother-in-law Chloe Rossi was outside sweeping in front of the store when she and a three of her deputies driving the other county owned SUVs full of officers drove through, lights flashing but no sirens. *Everyone will get the word we're up to something in about two minutes.* Trailing the rest, Mel waved at Chloe, but she didn't stop to talk to her.

They planned to fan out, knock on doors, figure out if anyone saw anything they'd admit to, even the driver of the car, and enlist the help of at least some of the property owners. Mounted search and rescue and the people who lived on the lands in question were better equipped to scour the woods, looking for the missing man or, heaven forbid, his body.

She knew Brian would be straight up with her and tell her if he saw the poachers and confronted them. She wasn't sure she wanted to know what he would have done when he got answers out of them that weren't to his liking.

She picked up speed and moved around a couple of her deputies as they moved aside a little, giving her more room to pass. Bypassing her aunt and uncle's closest neighbors on the frontage road, leaving them for one of the patrol groups now following, she turned up the steep slope of rutted mud and rock Brian dared to call a driveway. He purposely left it in awful shape, almost impassible in the spring and fall rains without four-wheel drive, to deter the city slickers looking for the lodge and winery a little further east. They had quickly grown tired of drunken tourists knocking on their door at all hours of the night, looking for the lodge and its associated cabins, getting their dogs all riled up.

Brian's preferred pickup truck was parked at the top of the hill, half behind the house, facing toward her. When she rounded the bend near the top of the hill and pulled her vehicle to a stop in front of his, she could see he was loading siding onto a flatbed trailer hitched to the back of the pickup. Her cousin Eric was in their four-car garage they used mostly for the equipment of their construction business, using a break to bend and cut the sheets.

"Aluminum?" she asked him, as she stepped out of her vehicle. "Didn't know you did much of that anymore."

"Not on new builds," Brian answered with a smile. "They're all vinyl these days. We're doing an addition to make a kitchen bigger and they want it to match the existing aluminum. I tried to tell 'em, they've got some sun fade that's going to show a difference. They didn't listen."

When Mel didn't respond, he went on, "I know this isn't a social call. I saw a couple of other vehicles go on by when I grabbed my gloves out of the cab a minute ago. What's up?"

Her cousin stopped what he was doing to join in their conversation. She didn't mince words with either of them. While they worked to strap down their load for the next day's work, she told them about the missing poacher and asked what they knew.

Brian waved a hand in the road's direction that was only a

slight upgrade from a dirt track. "You know I'm running people off here all the time, right?" Without waiting for her response, he went on, "That's mostly about that damn winery. Once bow season starts, I know there'll be hunters too, but it's been pretty quiet so far this summer."

"I'm not just talking up here around the house," she put in. "This guy would have been out on the back side of your property in some of your prime whitetail hunting area. When was the last time you were out there clearing paths or checking your tree stands to get ready for the season?"

He shrugged and glanced at her cousin. "Been a while for me, but he's been out there in the last week or so. You see anything?" he asked as he looked back at his son.

Eric shook his head. "Not real recently, like in the past few days. I've had to run Blake Wagner off my land a couple of times, though. He's been out in this area stealing and poaching whatever he could get his hands on."

Him again, Mel thought. *His name just keeps popping up.*

"Morels in the spring. 'Seng, I'm guessing is what he was after, earlier this month. I've got a patch out deep, off the back side of Mom and Dad's spread where mine joins it, that I've been cultivating for a couple of years. It's doing good, but it's mostly two root stuff this year. Next year, I'll get some three root pickings or better out of it...enough to pay my property taxes with, I suspect, if I can keep him and any other poachers out of it. Do you think he was out there, Mel? Maybe he saw those two and tangled with them. He tends to be territorial, whether or not it's his property."

She turned his question around. "Have you seen him out there this week, or seen him much at all, recently, honestly?"

"No, not recently. I busted him early in the month, like I said, but we all know that doesn't deter him. Let's be realistic. He might have given it a full twenty-four hours before he was back at it in the same area if he thought there was something out there to be had that was worth something or that he could eat off of for a time. You know as well as I do, he's taken game out of season when he was sure he wouldn't be caught by the wardens or you and your folks."

"Yeah, one of these days a property owner is going to catch him in the act, then I'm going to have a mess on my hands."

The two men were silent.

"How much of what's back there is yours? I thought the Amish bought most of that property when old man Lane died."

Brian grunted. "They did. Right out from under me. I bought ten acres from Lane for Eric's house before he died."

"It's more to the East," Eric said. "They own most of the land on the back property line. Been bringing down a lot of timber out there...logging, not for firewood. Maybe they saw something."

Mel thanked them and turned to leave just in time to see her family farm's Ranger UTV climbing up the drive with her mother behind the wheel. *Chloe got the word out fast.* She waved in her mom's direction, but she didn't wait for her. She knew Brian and Eric would tell her everything she was out there to find out.

~

Friday, September 30th
Press Briefing Room
Muskingum County Sheriff's Office

"Steve Hanford's body was found a mile and a tenth off SR 45 near Morelville, in a field currently used as a pasture, which was cleared from forest three years ago by members of the Gingrich Amish family. A pulling horse put in the pasture to feed appears to have found the corpse first and stood guard over it, keeping the turkey vultures away. When he couldn't be swayed back to the barn for work by the whistle of Matthew Gingrich, the old farmer stomped through the field to him and discovered Hanford."

Mel doubted the birds would have attempted to eat him, but the blood covering his shirt from the bullet wound on his chest probably attracted them when it was fresh. Now it was dry, and he was rotting.

Mel looked around. She knew she'd have to get her detectives out to comb the area more thoroughly, but she saw no evidence of a struggle. None that the horse hadn't trampled down, anyway. There were no tire tracks. There was no murder weapon, no obvious blood splatter. Nothing. She had her doubts they, whoever they were, even killed the man there. Her parents and the Rossi's had helped the department and mounted search and rescue comb the Lafferty's property and hundreds of acres of the surrounding area for two days. They'd found nothing.

Mel shook her head ruefully as she recalled Chloe spending every down minute trying to corner her and question her while her mother hovered nearby, hanging on every word.

Monday, October 3rd
Muskingum County Sheriff's Department

"Marc Salyers passed the polygraph," Shane Harding reported to Mel from just outside her door frame. "Doc says the certainty is pretty high that he's telling the truth."

Mel nodded at her detective and waved him in. "He's a poacher, but he never struck me as a killer. His demeanor is all wrong. He hardly acts like a criminal at all."

"What now?" he asked as he took a seat in her only visitor's chair.

She rubbed a hand in the hair at the back of her neck and thought about it. "Somebody took a shot at him with a .22. A varmint gun, and probably a .22 small pistol. Something little enough to carry and conceal until you're in range. He wasn't shot from a hundred yards. That part's not likely, anyway. Someone got up pretty close."

"Their driver, maybe?"

"We're pretty sure the driver was Salyers' wife, Rejean. She's on camera at the gas station in Philo. Janet went out and looked this morning when she got off the night shift. Not a big woman. Five feet tall, a hundred pounds, dripping wet. If she was the shooter, she sure didn't move him to where he was found."

"What are you thinking?"

"Potentially random? Someone who spotted them and stalked them, or at least him, waiting for an opportunity to steal his haul."

"Shot for ginseng." Shane shook his head. "How much do you really think he found and had on him?"

"We won't know unless we find his collection bag or we find the buyer for the killer," Mel said. "A lot of those buyers operate under the radar themselves, though. They know ninety-five percent of their product is stolen from private property or government land to begin with."

"What now?"

"We can hold Salyers a little longer on suspicion. In the meantime, we need to look at some of our other bad actors out that way."

"That's your area of expertise."

She sighed. "Unfortunately, yes, and there are more than a few of them. There's one I know I need to talk to anyway on an unrelated matter."

CHAPTER 14–PICKING BLAKE'S BRAIN

Hattie's Herbs and Oils
Morelville, Ohio

Blake Wagner gave Hattie a lopsided grin, showing off a couple of teeth stained from years of smoking and neglect. "I can't tell you how glad I am that there's going to be a local place for me to sell my 'seng. Those dealers that drive around buying it off of people just cheat us. The guy that's been working the county this season was the worst of the lot. I couldn't tell how, but he had his scale weighted somehow, for sure. I've been taking my stuff out of the county. Better prices." He raised an eyebrow at her.

Hattie shook her head in what she hoped looked like sympathy. The man made her uneasy, but she couldn't put a finger on why that was.

"When are you going to start buying?"

"As soon as I can officially get open for business. I'm waiting for the electrical inspector to come and sign off on everything."

"Thought you were open, since you've got a sign up and all. Season's about over."

She spread her hands. "I'd love to be open now, but I've got to follow the codes." *I need to put a coming soon notice out there and start locking up.*

Blake started talking, but Hattie went on as the door opened and Sheriff Crane and one of her deputies walked in. "I assure you," she was telling him, "I'm a licensed dealer. I got that taken care of with the state right away. Once I can start buying, I'll take fresh or dried ginseng, three or four prongs only, through the end of the year."

Blake didn't bother to turn to see the newcomers. Instead, he complained, "But, you can sell dried through March. That's the law."

Mel stepped to the counter, moving up next to Blake.

He glanced her way. "Sheriff." He dipped his head in acknowledgment. "Nothing illegal going on here to concern you. We were just talking about our future business dealings."

"That so?"

"Yes."

She nodded Hattie's way in acknowledgment, then turned back to Blake. She knew he wasn't stupid. Deciding the direct approach was the best option with him, she asked, "Where have you been picking these days?"

He scoffed. "I'm not going to tell you where my sweet spots are."

The deputy spoke up. "Look, Blake, we don't have any interest in tromping through the woods after roots. Not a one. We just want to know the general vicinity you've been hunting in."

"I've gotten permission for all the property I've been on."

As the deputy shook his head, Mel asked, "Been hunting in Blue Rock this year?"

It was a trap, but he saw it coming. "No. That's illegal without a permit. The state didn't issue any permits this year. They take an off year, every fourth year."

He leaned back against Hattie's counter, seemingly relishing his opportunity to pick Mel's brain for once. "This is really about those two poachers, isn't it, Sheriff?" He used her title like it pained him, sneering at her as he said it.

"Did you run into either of them out there?" she asked.

"Not that I recall. Just me and a bunch of critters out there. Lotta your precious whitetail."

"You never saw another human?"

"Just the property owners. I always double check with them before I go off on my way."

She shifted on her feet and crossed her arms, but she said nothing.

"I do this the right way, Mel," he said, reverting to the familiar with her. "I only pick ripe, and I replant the berries. People can't find my spots because I have a special way of doing things. Those two didn't get any of my stuff." He thumped his own chest. "I've got my honey holes out there and I take good care of them. I assure you, I ain't cheating nobody out of nothin'. I just like to dry some of my 'seng and spread out my income a little, through the winter…if I can find a dealer that'll take it."

Hattie found that odd. She knew from conversations with her aunt and Selma that he was a gunsmith. "Wouldn't the winter be a busy season for you? I mean, what with all the hunting. Aren't you a gunsmith, too?"

He stood up straight and half turned to look at her. "You've been checking up on me, have you?"

"You gave me your card…Well, you laid one on the counter when you came in," she said, taking a wild stab. She feigned giving it some thought, then reached under the edge of the register that wasn't even plugged in at that point. She rubbed her thumb across her fingers and let the card materialize. "Here it is." She flashed it at him.

He glanced at it and shrugged. "It's mine. Guess I don't remember, but you're right. I would have just laid it on the counter. I don't do handshakes. Too many germs."

The deputy had a coughing fit that stopped only when Mel shot him a look.

Hattie looked at Blake's dirt-stained hands and stifled a shuddering shoulder cringe herself.

Faye drove by Hattie's shop headed toward the farm. She slowed when she saw both Blake's Gator and her daughter's county SUV parked outside.

So odd that they're all in there when it isn't even open for business yet. She debated stopping and going in, but she knew Mel would think she was interfering in her case if she was in there talking with either Blake or Hattie about Delores.

That Hattie. I don't trust her. I don't care what Chloe says...feels. "Auras. Humph."

Inside, Blake continued to ignore Mel's questions and changed the subject to morel mushrooms. "What are you doing with those? Anything?"

"I have some dried ones on hand right now to sell once I'm open for business, but not much since they aren't in season," Hattie said.

"It's okay. I'll bring lots in for you, in the spring."

Blake turned toward Mel and sneered. "Sheriff." He shook his head. "I'd like to say it's always a pleasure, but it ain't." With that, he turned and walked out of the shop.

Mel watched him go, then directed her gaze back to Hattie. "I'm going to tell you right now, he's bad news. Ninety-nine percent of what he'll bring you will be stolen off private property or out of Blue Rock without a permit."

"What should I do when he comes in, then?"

Mel ran a hand through her hair. "That's just it. There's not much you can do. Be fair with him or he'll ride you. Don't trust him with any sort of credit account or anything like that and if anyone comes in complaining about him, you call me."

Mel unbuttoned a pocket of her uniform shirt and took a card out. She wrote a number on the back and handed it to Hattie. "That's my cell number. Call me, not the station. If I'm not around the area anyway, I'll get someone down here right away."

Hattie stroked Freya's fur as she reflected on her first real interaction with Blake. "I find him totally lacking," she whispered to the cat. "I could feel his shadiness even before the Sheriff said anything."

Freya ducked Hattie's hand and skittered away a few feet along the counter-top, then sat and licked at a paw.

"Yes," Hattie finished to the air, "he's shady and I'm going to keep a close eye on him." She squeezed her eyes closed and conjured his image in her head. She saw him inside what she presumed was the interior of his home, but then he wasn't. The image in her mind's eye shifted to him at the store as something went on at his home. Her eyes flew open. "Something involving the sheriff!"

She picked up Mel's card. "I didn't conjure this one, Freya, but it looks like it's the one I'll be keeping." She tucked the card into her pocket, then moved toward the front door. Freya jumped down and followed her.

"Let's call it a day before we have any more unsavory types in here, shall we?"

Freya purred in response.

CHAPTER 15-ARREST

Tuesday, October 4th
Morelville, Ohio

Hattie watched out her aunt Bridget's front window as three police cruisers and Mel Crane's county SUV made the turn off the main road and continued toward Blake's home. She jumped up from her seat on the couch, spilling her aunt's old cat off her lap.

Bridget looked at her over the top of the half glasses she used for reading and her close up knitting. "What's got you all fired up suddenly?"

"I've just remembered I need to fetch something at the store." The older woman gave her a strange look, but she brushed it off. "I won't be but a minute."

As she hustled down out to the corner and crossed the main road, she could see the police vehicles arrayed across the front of Blake's home. *If you could call it that. Run down hovel is more like it.* She turned away from the scene and glanced down at the store, still a half a block away. Blake's gator was parked right outside. *At least my visions never lie to me.*

INSIDE, Blake was ordering Chloe and Faye about as they made him a Dagwood sandwich from several lunch meats and cheeses they needed to slice.

He paused long enough to nod Hattie's way.

She gave him her best smile as she told him, "You might want to hold off on that."

"Pardon?" Faye asked.

Hattie pointed at Blake. "I was talking more to him."

Faye dropped a chunk of ham into position on the slicer, but she didn't start it.

"And why is that?" he asked.

"You've got the yellowish house with white trim just up Market Street, right?"

"What about it?"

"You've got visitors." She stifled a grin and shrugged at him instead.

His eyes narrowed. "Come again?"

"There are several cops at your house."

Chloe threw Faye a glance that Hattie caught.

Massive sandwich forgotten; Blake focused on her. "Cops? What did you do? Yesterday, I told you and the sheriff that my stuff is legal.

"I did nothing at all," Hattie said. "I just noticed them pulling up out there as I was walking down here. Thought you'd want to know."

He brushed past her and rushed out of the store without another word. The three women watched as he started the gator and gunned the engine as he tore away from the curb and up the street.

"No great loss of business there," Chloe said to Faye as she watched her return the ham to the deli case.

As she wiped her hands on a towel, Faye eyed Hattie. "What's really going on? I saw both him and Mel parked down by your shop yesterday. Now this."

Hattie feigned a shrug. "Beats me. He was trying to sell me ginseng, but I'm not even open for business yet. I got the impression she stopped in to roust him about something, and she told me to be careful of anything he brings me. Other than that—"

"He's bad news," Chloe said.

"So I'm told."

Faye nodded along in agreement. "Believe it. Now, I have to wonder what's going up there. Do you think it's about the coins?" she asked the other two women.

"Or that dead guy," Hattie added.

"Or Delores," Chloe put in as she recalled her conversation about visions with Beth.

Muskingum County Sheriff's Department

BLAKE GLARED AT MEL. "Doing the questioning yourself, eh? Don't trust your detectives to get it right, Sheriff?"

"A man is dead, Mr. Wagner. Shot."

"That man everyone's been hunting for? The poacher?"

"Why don't you tell me everything you know about him?" It was more a demand than a question.

"I've got nothing for you."

"I have information that says you were in the same area as

the two poachers were the day one of them, Steve Hanford, went missing."

"First, I don't even know those two guys or know of them other than what I've heard around town as everyone searched for the one that came up missing. Second, it sounds like you're accusing me of being out there poaching, too."

"Can you account for your whereabouts over the past week?"

"Week? You're really reaching there, Sheriff. Every minute of every day? No. I mean, I can, but it won't make a difference to you or anybody else. I live alone. I work alone doing stuff for other people they send me out and about to do. They don't go with me. What would be the point of that?"

Mel shifted in her chair and changed lines of questioning at the same time. "Dolores Chappel's death may not have been by natural causes."

"May not?" he scoffed.

"There are some anomalies."

"So?"

"Your fingerprints were found in her house."

"Every time something goes down in Morelville, you come after me. All you ever have is circumstantial."

"Fingerprints?"

He was still stuck on the dead poacher. "Who says I was in the same area as that guy? Your aunt or uncle?"

Mel didn't respond.

"Look, I was out there doing some site surveying for the Amish. I might have crossed onto your cousin's property a time or two. There aren't many markers out there, after all."

"Site surveying?"

"Helping them mark their property." He sneered. "Seems they've had some run-ins with their *neighbors*. They want to play fair with your kin folk out there."

"And they hired *you* to help them?"

"I know what you're thinking. I'm not a surveyor. Not officially."

"There's no other kind, Blake. You have to have a license to set property lines in this county...in this state."

"Well, that's not exactly how it went down," He backpedaled. "Anyway, that was a month ago, not around the time that guy was found. As for Delores, I've been down there to have stuff notarized, Sheriff, as has half the village. I can't even remember when I was down there last, but it had to be before she went to jail. No reason for me to be there since then."

His sudden change of subject caught her off guard. She stood and leaned over the table a little to speak more directly to him. "Seems like we have a lot to talk about with regard to Mr. Hanford and with Delores Chappel."

He tried to rock back in the chair, but he didn't get far since it was bolted to the floor. He glowered instead. "I guess I'll be calling my lawyer and he'll want to know exactly where you found my prints, so you may as well tell me now."

When Mel didn't answer him, he claimed, "The only thing I believe I've ever touched at her place, aside from the door handles, would be her little writing desk in the kitchen where she does all her notary stuff. She's short. It's really low. I always have to lean way over to sign stuff she's notarizing for me."

She noted his use of the present tense. She knew he'd been at her funeral, but he was still talking about her as if she was alive. "What's the last thing you recall having notarized?"

"Really? What do you think?"

"Humor me."

"I'm a gunsmith. I'm licensed to sell guns. That's a license I want to keep, by the way. Can't do that if I'm out there committing felonies, now can I?"

When Mel didn't respond, he went on. "Most of what I have her do is notarize bills of sale when buyers require them. I hate going in there, you know? It's always hot and smells like fuel oil. I do my business and I get out. Spend as little time there as possible."

His explanation made sense, and Mel couldn't really argue with him about the smell and not wanting to spend a lot of time there. To him, she shrugged in what she hoped appeared to be indifference, but she mentally shook her head because where he said they would be was exactly where they found his prints. She pushed him anyway. "Where were you a week ago today?"

"Last Tuesday?"

She nodded.

"Not in to see Delores, if that's what you're asking. Figured she was still in jail."

"None of the Chappels told you she was out?"

"I steer clear of them...other than her, when I need her, anyway." He stroked the scruff on his chin, appearing to be in deep thought. He opened, after several long seconds, with, "It's hard telling. I've been doing a lot of work for Kent Gross, and I know I was with him or working on his property part of that day."

"About what time frame?

Blake threw up a hand. "Most of the morning, starting about, say, 8:00?" It came out as more of a question. "You'll have to check with him."

CHAPTER 16–CAN'T KEEP HOLD OF HIM

Friday, October 7th

Chloe watched out the front window of the store as Blake went by on the state route on his noisy Gator. She shook her head. "Thought he was in jail," she turned and said to Faye.

"Was that Blake, just now? Yeah. I did too." She swiped a rag back and forth across the countertop and shook her head, too. "Can't believe Mel would let him go."

"Speaking of Mel. She just turned in. She had to have passed him."

"Is she coming in here?"

Chloe shrugged, but Faye's question was soon answered.

Mel entered, nodded at Chloe, and said, "Hey," to her mother.

"Hi yourself," Faye said. "You're home early."

"Slow day. Looks like things are slow in here, too."

"To say the least," Chloe said. She wasted no time getting to the topic burning in her mind. "We just saw Blake Wagner go by. We thought he was in jail."

Mel gave her mother-in-law a tight-lipped grin. "I can only

hold him so long." She moved toward the meat freezer. "I need something I can thaw quick and fix for Dana and the baby for dinner. Hannah's in class, and it's nice out, so I'm going to grill."

Faye jumped in. "You're changing the subject. You can't tell me you didn't have evidence to hold Blake."

Mel turned back to her mother. "All I'll say is this, because it's an ongoing investigation; he appears to have an alibi for the time of Delores's death, which has not been established as anything but natural causes. We can't prove anyone else was there recently."

"Yet. You can't prove it was anything but natural causes, yet."

Mel sighed audibly. "Everything that happens is not a crime."

"But you're still investigating him, right?" Chloe asked.

"*I'm* still investigating. *My department* is still investigating all the crimes and alleged crimes, yes."

"What about the mess down there, Melissa?" her mother asked, glossing over Mel's obvious implication to stay out of her business. "That's not evidence of a crime?"

"Look you two, for all we know, Delores made the mess herself as she was going through the stages of her heart attack."

"What about those ginseng poachers?" Chloe asked. "You don't think he had something to do with them? And maybe it's all tied together."

"The death of Delores and the murder of Steve Hanford aren't connected. You two are going to have to trust me on that."

Faye said to Chloe, as they prepared to close the store, "I'm not buying that nothing spooked Delores. Even in the throes of chest pain, she was the type who would just sit quietly and wait for it to pass. She wasn't a real active person. Quite the opposite. But the other thing about her was, she wasn't one to leave a disorganized mess. She wasn't what the kids would call a neat freak, but she was hyper organized with her things."

"Do you really think Blake has a solid alibi?" Chloe asked as she turned the open sign on the door around to show closed.

"Melissa says he does. I have to believe her about that."

"So, if not Blake, then who?"

"I really think we should focus on Hattie." Chloe baulked, but Faye waved a hand at her. "Hear me out." As she tugged the cover over the slicer, she said, "First, she always seems to be in the right place at the wrong time. She's Bridget's niece. It's obvious she's on good terms with Selma, so she probably has been to her home. I can't quite make the Delores piece fit, but since her shop is so close and she's renting from the Chappells, maybe she saw Delores there or found out she was there through the Chappells."

Chloe shook her head. "No. It's not Hattie. It can't be. What could she possibly have to gain here?"

"Money."

"She doesn't need money, Faye. Hattie's one of the highest paid actresses in Hollywood."

"She's not in Hollywood anymore. Maybe she ran through all her money."

"Possibly. Let's put that aside for the moment. She also had no reaction at all to any news about Delores being surrounded by a mess of her coins other than what appeared to be the surprise we all felt."

"She's an actress, Chloe. You just said that."

Chloe approached the counter and asked softly, "What about Beth's vision, Faye?"

Faye turned off the lights in the deli case as she answered. "I don't buy that for a minute. Beth probably saw Delores and the rest was a dream that came from that. I also think we've been lucky so far that Beth doesn't know what's happened."

"If she doesn't already know, and that's a big if, maybe we should tell her. Or, better yet, have Mel tell her."

"What purpose do you think that would serve?"

"Mel might be able to put her mind at ease. And, vision or not, if she really saw something, she may have information that could help Mel nail Blake, after all."

"Or Hattie," Faye said with a shrug.

"Or whoever."

CHAPTER 17—COIN CHAOS

Saturday, October 8th

Hattie shook her head at the mess. She could tell Delores had been a pack rat of sorts, but an orderly one. "A place for everything and everything in its place," she muttered.

In the kitchen, where it appeared everything had once been stored in rolling chests of drawers made from plastic, chaos reigned. The clear tubs that made up the drawers of each unit had been pulled out of their housings, emptied and the contents stacked about. Burnished wood display cases meant to contain full collections of rare coins were piled haphazardly on the kitchen table next to a mound of coins individually cased in plastic holders and cardboard sleeves with round, see-through windows made for exactly the purpose they were serving.

To Hattie, aside from the mess, the place had a bad vibe. She began her work with a complex cleansing ritual that took something out of her but made her feel better about the task ahead. Once the ritual was done, she pulled on some latex gloves and picked a few coins off one of the piles. *A buffalo nickel and an Indian head penny, both in pretty decent condition.* She'd never been interested in the hobby herself, but she knew condition was important to collectors almost as much as rarity was.

The paperwork strewn about the table and across the floor was the other sign to her that Delores' killer had been looking for something specific, *like a Carson City stash of coins, maybe?*

She gathered most of the paperwork and sorted through it, quickly realizing that Delores had been quite old-fashioned in her approach to the hobby. There were mint and distributor catalogs, collection subscription documents, invoices and packing slips. *Mail order? Who still does this?*

She glanced around her and then did a quick scan of the other rooms. No computer. The only semi-modern piece of technology in the place was a flat screen TV that had a plastic dust cover over it where it sat on what looked to be a microwave cart off to one side of the kitchen. *They were after something specific they knew was here.*

She took a deep breath, dug down deep within herself and waved her hands about while using her mind to will the myriad of coins back into their boxes and drawers. The process, even using magic, took several minutes and drained much of her energy, but she ended up with a neat stack of the wooden display cases, each matched up with the appropriate invoices and other paperwork.

Hattie took a seat and went through each case and the related documentation by hand. It wasn't long before she realized only a few of the sets were complete. Most were not. Not even close. The incomplete sets were often one to three coins shy of being finished.

She looked at the bills. *Every four to six weeks. Sometimes eight to ten. Put them on a subscription plan and string them along for life.*

About halfway through the stack of stuff, she found an empty box; empty that is except for the packing slips, invoices, and certificates of authenticity from Littleton Coin Company certifying the coins delivered to Delores as being authentic Carson City issues from 1881.

Bingo! She went through the invoices line by line. She should have had four coins out of a five-coin set. There were none.

Hattie didn't know the street value or the collector value of what was missing, but she could see the invoice prices for the four coins that had been shipped were well over $2,000.00. *Still, hardly worth killing someone over, unless you're really desperate.* They can't be easy to move, and they were ungraded, so their value probably wasn't close to what she paid, she thought.

She knew she had to report what she'd found, but she also knew she couldn't say anything about the other thefts to the police. Instead, she took out her phone and snapped pictures of the invoices to save to show her aunt and her aunt's friends. *Maybe they'll convince Aunt Bridget to go to the police now.*

Once she put her phone away, she got down to the real work of cleaning without using her magic. She knew the police and the Chappells would suspect something if she finished too quickly. She didn't need that kind of scrutiny and speculation. Not now.

"I showed the Chappells what I found down there. They called the police, so I told them too." Hattie confided in Chloe as the older woman kept a watchful eye on two kids pawing through the store candy racks. "I didn't say anything about the other thefts, though I probably should have because I don't think she believed me."

"Did you talk to Mel, dear?"

"Oh, no. Not her. A detective. I don't think I could have kept the other stuff from the Sheriff. She seems like a tough one."

Chloe smiled and shook her head. "You don't know her very well."

"So, now what do we do? I mean, I feel like I should push Aunt Bridget forward. Whoever took those coins killed for them."

"Or they got surprised," Chloe said. "Everyone around here thought Delores was in prison, remember?"

"If you're just out to steal a few coins, why would you not just get out of there when you realize you're not alone? Go back another time?"

Chloe had to admit, she had a good point.

Stanley Chappell called on Mel at home later that afternoon, frustrating Mel because her mother was there helping with Hannah's teething, cranky toddler, Jef. Dana had taken Hannah to the dentist at a Saturday clinic for an exam that was the first in the young, former Amish young woman's life. There was no way to escape the prying eyes and ears of her mother given the toddler's always present desire to be anywhere Mel was when she was at home.

"Who's this little guy?" Stanley asked as he attempted to squat to the toddler's level.

Mel held Stanley's arm, giving him an assist as he rose again. "Do you know Hannah Yoder, that runs the bakery? He's her son. They live here with me."

As he moved toward Dana's favorite armchair, he said, "My, yes. Love those cookies she makes. At my age, I really shouldn't eat them at all, but...well, at my age, who cares? I'm going to die, anyway."

"Oh, now!" Faye scoffed. "You're not that old."

He ignored her obvious attempt at flattery. "I was Delores'

older brother, Faye. She was eighty. Anyway, she's the reason I'm here."

"I figured," Mel said. She looked pointedly at her mother, but Faye didn't budge. She called Jef to her as she took a seat herself.

"Hattie Novak, who's renting the old Stark place next to Delores' place, gave your detective a statement yesterday," Stanley said.

"I've seen it."

"If there's any chance at all, Delores was spooked by someone and that caused her heart attack, I want her death looked into a lot more closely. She may have gone to jail for her crimes, but she didn't deserve to die the way she did."

"What was Hattie doing in Delores' house, Stanley?" Faye asked.

Mel shot her mother another look, but she ignored it too and fussed over the toddler.

"She's opening some kind of store in the Stark place. While she waits for county stuff to go through - you know how that goes - she's been trying to stay busy. She went in there and worked on cleaning up the mess for us. Between the coins and your people dusting the place—" He spread his hands.

Mel called her niece Beth over from next door after dinner. As they worked on her dirt bike in Mel's garage, Mel asked her about her vision involving Delores.

"You believe me about my vision, Aunt Mel?"

"Honey, I'll be honest. I don't know what to believe. I'm just trying to look at everything."

"That woman is dead."

"Delores? Yes. I'm sorry to have to tell you that."

"It wasn't a question. I know she is. Everyone's been talking about it all over."

"Here in the village? Yeah. Probably."

"Everywhere. On the bus. At school. It's creepy. They're all being so morbid about it."

"Was it morbid? Your vision, I mean?"

Beth was silent for a long time. Mel tinkered with a wrench, leaving the teenager to her thoughts.

"I don't really know how to describe it. Everything was so dark in my dream, except for this blue light."

"Blue light?"

"Yeah, like from a TV or something."

"Inside the house?"

"Inside the kitchen. There was a TV on, but there was no show. The screen was all blue like when Cole turns off the TV at our house but forgets to shut off the cable, like he always does."

Mel thought about the covered flat screen in the kitchen. She put her wrench down, abandoning all pretext of working on the dirt bike. "Beth, think about this very closely, okay? Did you see a TV on in your dream...your vision, or do you think you saw the glow of it at night, another time, for real?"

"I don't have to think about it. It was part of the dream."

"Okay." Mel sighed.

"You know that little stand Hannah has with the plastic drawers you can sort of see in that's in Jef's room? The one where she keeps his diapers and creams and his bath stuff?"

"Yes."

"She had a bunch of those in her kitchen. At least five or six. Maybe more. And little wood boxes. Well, not tiny. Like that jewelry box thing Lance has on his dresser that he calls a man's box."

Mel laughed, but Beth wasn't trying to be funny and frowned at her. "I'm sorry. Go on."

"There were no legs on the boxes, not like with that jewelry box Mom has that sits on top of her dresser that's smaller than Lance's but thicker…deeper. And there were coins, and papers, and little packets everywhere."

"Have you ever been inside that house, Beth?"

"No, Aunt Mel. I've never even been in her yard. Everyone always said she was mean. I stayed away."

As she went back over the list of things she saw in her vision, Kris ambled toward them.

"Was anyone there?" Mel got in before Kris reached them.

"The woman that lives there."

"No one else?"

"Just her."

When her mother stepped through the open bay door, Beth clammed up, but Kris didn't push to know what they'd been talking about. Instead, she said to her daughter, "You've got church in the morning, and you volunteered to read, remember? You better go work through the verses a couple of times. I'll be in to listen in a few minutes."

"Yes ma'am," the teenager agreed. She sketched a wave at her grandmother who was leaving Mel's house, and she left.

Faye joined her daughters in the garage. She said, "Dana's eating what I put aside for her, and Hannah skipped dinner, but she insisted on giving Jef his bath herself, so she's not too awful traumatized from the dentist."

Mel grinned.

"Now, what was that all about?" Faye asked. She flapped a hand toward the house Kris and her husband Lance owned next door to Mel's house.

"We were just working on her bike," Mel said.

Faye clucked her tongue at her twin who was older than her sister by a few minutes. "There's no grease on your hands, Melissa."

"And I asked her about her vision."

Faye made a show of rolling her eyes, but Kris grew concerned. "What...what did she say?"

"I was skeptical, but other than one minor detail, she nailed the scene in the house."

"So, what does that mean?" Kris asked.

Faye interrupted. "You don't think she went over there for some reason and saw her?" Faye asked.

"No, I don't. Not at all. Believe me, I asked. She looked me straight in the eye and she didn't waver."

"I feel so bad now," Kris said. "To be saddled with something like that...with these visions for life." She spread her hands in front of her. "What are we going to do? This could be so traumatizing for her."

CHAPTER 18–REVELATIONS AND QUESTIONS

Tuesday Morning, October 11th
Morelville General Store

Faye swiped absently at the front counter with a damp rag.

"Something on your mind?" Chloe asked.

Faye shook her head, but she wiped a little harder.

"Come on. I know you better than that. What's up?"

She sighed and gave in. "Mel talked to Beth last night about her vision of Delores."

"Really?"

Faye simply nodded.

"Well, it doesn't surprise me she talked to her. Any idea what came of it?" *She knows. She wouldn't be dwelling on it so hard if she didn't.* Chloe tried to lean against the counter and appear casual, but she felt awkward and drew herself back up, then leaned across the counter toward her friend, instead.

"Mel said she pretty accurately described the chaos inside the house, and she says Beth swears she hasn't been in there and isn't the cause of the mess."

"No details, though?"

Faye tossed her head. "Official police investigation, remember?"

"That's right. Of course." *Drat!* She did her best to keep her composure because she didn't want to annoy her friend at being overly curious about her granddaughter.

Faye brought Beth up again, herself. "Do you suppose she'll always have these visions? I mean, mine stopped back in the day, before...Well, never mind about that."

Chloe decided to tread carefully. *There's more to the story of Beth, I'm sure, but I'm not sure Faye realizes it.* "I can't answer that, sweetie. Yours went away, maybe hers will too."

Faye said, "That's not all that happened last night." She paused, then said, "There's something else I need to tell you about," when the bell over the door rang and Hattie entered the store. Faye clammed up.

"Hi there," Chloe said. "Anything we can help you with today?" She shot Faye a look.

"Can you put a rush on the code inspector for me? Otherwise, I just need a bag of ice today."

"The county inspectors?" Chloe asked.

"Yes. For electrical. I can't open until the new fuse box and all the new wiring has been signed off on." She threw up a hand. "The whole deal is pretty frustrating."

Chloe touched her shoulder and commiserated, "I'm right there with you. Why, I never thought we'd get this place up to code and open when we bought it. Then," she waved toward the back of the store, "we tried to put a little nail salon back there, and we couldn't get the county inspector to sign off on the pedicure chairs with their footbaths."

Hattie scrunched up her face. "The part that's a bakery now?"

Faye jumped in. "Yeah. She tried to put the nail place in there first. Jumped through even more hoops when she put commercial ovens in there and sold it to Hannah instead. There's only one county electrical inspector, and he's never in a rush."

The bell over the door sounded again as Hattie said, "Maybe he'll take a bribe?" Her tone was laced with humor, but Faye recoiled at the statement, recovering only when Mildred Penny approached the group of them.

She and Chloe both turned to her and said hello at the same time.

Mildred said, "I didn't expect to see you both here." She nodded to Chloe and to Faye.

"I help part time," Faye explained. "Keeps me busy. We don't see you in here often."

The other woman gave a half shrug. "We were always running to take care of Elias's mother, so I guess we did most of our shopping along the way. Philo mostly. Anyway, Elias is off to the estate lawyer today and I find I need a can of cream of mushroom soup. I don't want to drive all the way up there for that if I don't have to. Do you have any?"

"Certainly. Right this way." Chloe led her around the row of shelves that divided the front part of the store in two and showed her the soups, then left her to make her choice of the two off-brands they carried. She scurried back to the register to catch Hattie before she left.

She nudged her with a shoulder and whispered, "I saw you were down there at Delores's place over the weekend. Find anything interesting?"

"I...I was just cleaning it up for the Chapells."

Faye's eyes narrowed. "Cleaning, huh?"

"Yes. It needed done. There was the mess, of course, and then fingerprint dust everywhere. They were going to pay for a service to go in and do it, but that would have been really expensive. Since I'm at loose ends for the moment, I offered to do it."

"Free?" Faye asked.

Chloe shot her a warning look, but Faye didn't even hazard a glance her way.

"No. Stanley insisted I take a payment, and I could use the money, but I didn't charge him anywhere near what that service was going to charge."

Wait, what? "Didn't you leave Hollywood with a little cash tucked away?" Chloe asked, her innate nosiness getting the better of her.

"I did, but I've been sinking a lot of my savings into the shop, preparing it and acquiring stock for it. I won't get a royalty check from the show again for a while. Besides, like I said, I'm just trying to stay busy. There's only so much I can do around the house for Aunt Bridget."

Mildred approached the counter with a can of mushroom soup and a bottle of ranch salad dressing. Chloe and Hattie stood by quietly and watched while Faye rang her out. She left with murmured thanks and a faint wave.

Faye shook her head. "That poor dear. I don't know what she sees in Elias."

"Faye Crane!" Chloe called her out. "What brought that on?"

"He's so...so...what's the word for full of himself?"

"Pompous?" Hattie offered.

Faye pointed at her. "Yes! Thank you. That's it. Pompous. And she's a sweetheart, serves his every whim."

Chloe thought about how Jesse treated Faye, but she held her tongue.

Hattie said, "I've got to get going. I promised Aunt Bridget I'd be right back with this ice. She's been through enough with the thefts and then Delores dying and all, and now she's gone and twisted her ankle. It's swelling faster than the ice maker on her old fridge can keep up."

"Oh, dear," Faye said. "Anything we can do?"

"Besides the ice? No. It's just a twist. She did it yesterday, out running around, doing more than she should have been."

Chloe clucked her tongue, then said, "Not to change the subject, but it seems to me like the police have forgotten Bridget and Selma in the whole mix of things with Delores."

Hattie nodded in agreement.

Faye reminded them both, "Mel went after Blake. She wouldn't have done that just on our say so."

Chloe didn't want to give herself away, but she said to the other two women, "Mel must have gone and talked to Selma."

Faye defended her daughter. "Melissa is doing the best she can with what little she has to work with."

Hattie admitted, "I figured something out while I was down there cleaning that might move everything along." She told them about the missing Carson City coins from Delores Chapell's collection. "I made a report to the police, so I figure Mel will really be on the case now." She tipped her head to Faye.

"I have to confess," Faye said. "Stanley came by Melissa's house last night while I was there and talked to her. I kind of already had an inkling about what you just told us."

Chloe slapped a hand to her heart. "And you didn't tell me?"

"I was about to. We were talking about Beth, and then I started to bring it up, but everyone came in."

"I'm sorry to keep you," Chloe said to Hattie, "but do you have any idea what the value was of the coins from the paper-work you saw?"

Hattie told them how she thought the coin subscriptions Delores had worked and what she'd paid for the Carson City coins she found invoices for but no coins. "I figure, so PCS and Littleton, the two companies she dealt with for the Carson City coins, could make money, she was paying more than the value of the coins and the presentation cases in total. Probably quite a bit more, but the coins would appreciate over time, and they've been coming one at a time, every few months over a few years."

"Were the coins graded?" Chloe asked.

Hattie shrugged. "They were mostly from sets she mail ordered from distributors. How would I tell?"

Chloe explained what she knew about slabbing.

"If that's how they'd look," Hattie said, "it doesn't appear they were slabbed, judging by other stuff Delores had from the same dealer that was left behind by whoever took the Carson City stuff."

Chloe looked at Faye. "What do you think our next move should be?"

"Well, if they didn't come slabbed, and they weren't done later, that means Elias probably hadn't been asked to do any of that sort of work for her. That puts his connection into question, so what other connections, besides Blake, are there?"

"Someone...us probably," Chloe glanced back at Faye, "should talk to Bridget, see if we can pick her brain and maybe find a link we may have missed before."

"Do you want me to be there?" Hattie asked.

"Let me think on that one," Faye said before Chloe could answer. "Meanwhile, we have some other people we still need to talk to."

"Like Kent Gross," Chloe said. "I was supposed to find a reason to talk to him. And Jason. You were going to talk to him."

"I talked to Jason a while back, before the funeral for Delores, actually." Faye offered. "I was trying to talk money with him. I certainly didn't get that. I got little out of him then at all beyond him having supposed sentimental reasons for wanting to restore the old Baptist church."

"Did you believe him about his reasons?" Hattie asked.

Faye thought about it. "I did then, but that was before we saw him and Kent acting weird at the funeral."

To herself, Chloe thought, *I really want to talk to Hattie about Beth. She's younger, more relatable. I don't want to step on Faye's toes, though. She's already riled up about Hattie. No sense stirring that pot anymore.*

Chloe asked Hattie what she thought about Kent.

The younger woman said, "The only experience I have with him is during and right after the Sertoma meeting. He seemed to be in an awful big hurry to get to Jason's new business then."

"Would you want to go with me to talk to him? I think we would be less suspicious to him if you went with me and we talked about something to do with your membership or something else to do with Sertoma, like you sponsor an event, maybe, and we work our way around to talking to him about what we really want to know."

"That's a good idea," Faye said, surprising Chloe.

"You're okay with it if I take Hattie with me instead of you?"

Hattie gave Chloe a questioning look.

"It makes sense. I mean, you could ask him flat out about his intentions for the church, but what if he really isn't involved in that and all the business with Jason is about something else? I mean, they're talking about Sertoma purchasing the land, so it has to be something; but what? He's a talker. Get him talking."

Chloe addressed Hattie. "You could ask him about putting up a booth at the mushroom festival for your business because the mushroom festival is something that Sertoma sponsors and helps to run. That's in the late spring."

"That's a good idea," Hattie said. "And it won't cost me any money right now. I'm afraid he might jump quickly on the sponsorship thing. Like I said, my cash flow is a little light right now."

"You two talk to him, meanwhile I'll talk to Bridget." Faye paused. "Check that. First, I think I'll try to talk to Molly."

Hattie spread her hands. "Molly?"

"The postmaster."

"I know who she is, but why?"

"She'd be one of the few to know Delores was getting coins via mail order. She'd know if anyone else was too," Faye said. "And maybe she's on the take. She knows a lot about everyone in the village, but she doesn't live here. What do we really know about her?"

Chloe scrunched her face. Ignoring the last bit, she asked, "But if she knew about anyone else, would she tell you about them? She's always been a stickler for the rules."

"I'll figure it out. That's the plan," Faye said.

Hattie laughed. "Hey! That's my line."

"Pardon?" Faye looked confused.

"One of her catch phrases on the show," Chloe said.

"What is?"

Chloe and Hattie both said in unison, "That's the plan!"

Later That Day

The two women got a little more than they bargained for when they stepped into the office Kent had built out in a corner of one of the large pole barns on his property. Jason was in there with him. The latter did not seem happy to see them, but Kent greeted them warmly with, "Ladies." He dipped his head. "To what do I owe the pleasure?"

"We came to talk about Sertoma," Chloe said as Hattie nodded in agreement. "Is this a bad time?"

"Not at all," Kent said. He waved a hand at Jason. "We were just discussing the same thing."

Jason sunk a little lower in his chair and glowered at Chloe.

"Wonderful, but frankly, we'll be quick," she said, ignoring the other man. "I left Faye by herself to run the store. We're not here about what that committee is set up to look into. Not directly, if that's what you think."

"Sit. Sit." Kent waved his hand toward a sofa and moved from behind his desk, dragging his wheeled chair along with him.

Chloe gave Hattie a look and moved that way somewhat reluctantly. *I really don't want to be here long.*

"First," Hattie began without moving from where she stood, "was my membership approved?"

"You saw that at the meeting."

"You gave me an application to fill out, which I returned to you. I've heard nothing."

Kent waved a hand. "You passed the vote. The application is just a formality. We forward that to the national organization. They'll get you all set up. You'll get something in the mail soon, I imagine."

"Is that really why you're here?" Jason asked.

Hattie turned and shot him a look. "I beg your pardon. Have we met?"

"You saw me at the Sertoma meeting."

"But I don't know you."

"Everyone in town knows you, though. Big movie star."

Her voice took on a more modest, less questioning tone as she told him, "I've never even been in a movie. I was on television, and I'm hardly a star. A few commercials and I got lucky to get a supporting role on a popular sitcom."

Her spiel did not sway him. "So, why are you here?"

Hattie started to respond, but Chloe waved a hand, drawing her attention. "Hattie is working hard to get all of her licensing, and permits and such in place, and she hopes to have it all done before the next festival, so she has questions about booths and such that I can't answer—"

"Faye Crane could have," Jason said, unhelpfully. "You all

hang together."

Chloe plowed ahead. "Possibly, but probably not. We had a proposal for you," she said as she nodded to Kent, "but I can see this isn't the right time." She stood, looked at Hattie, and tipped her head toward the door.

Hattie turned to go but wasn't able to take a step before Kent called out, "Now hold on here. Jason, calm down. Let these ladies talk."

His words sent a chill down Chloe's spine that she did her best to mask.

"You know why they're really here," Jason went on. "It's about that church, the same as we've been talking about. I'm not stupid."

Hattie stepped in. "Jason, I'm new here. I'm not on top of most things. All I know about that church, I learned at the meeting. That was less about the church and more about the land it sits on, and about you wanting Sertoma to buy it from the township."

"The township has already told the committee they won't sell," Kent said.

"Say what?" Chloe asked as she plopped sat back down in the chair she'd vacated.

Kent leaned back in his leather desk chair, his hands spread. "The committee members didn't waste any time going around, making inquiries. Small town, you know."

"Village," Jason corrected.

"That's what we were talking about," Kent continued. "The township says the land is not for sale at any price, to any buyer, community organization or not."

"Hmm. Wonder why that is?" Chloe asked.

Jason said, "One word, thanks to you and Faye: preservation. If they don't sell, no one can raze that church and then build anything else on that land."

"Makes sense," Hattie said. "But my understanding is the church is being preserved."

"Yes," Chloe answered. "Faye and I got the old opera house restored, and now we're working on that church. A church that means a lot to a lot of folks in this community. Jason, here has been letting us do it." She decided not to mention what Faye had told her about his supposed motives, hoping to draw him out and either confirm them or get a different story.

"It means a lot to my family too," Jason admitted. "That's why I bought it. I've just never had the money to put in it."

Hattie asked, "Were you ever considering tearing it down?" She glanced quickly at Chloe, then refocused on him.

"No. I want to see it stay there. It just needs a lot of work." He held a hand out toward Kent. "He's willing to put some money in it, but with the township owning the land, they can dictate what we ultimately do on it."

"And what is that, Mr. Gross?" Chloe asked him.

Kent inhaled deeply. "I'm planning a little development for land I own in the village," he divulged. "I know there's been a lot of speculation about my intentions. They're all good, I assure you."

Her brow furrowed, Chloe asked, "What sort of development?"

"And the church figures into that, how?" Hattie added.

"This is all in the early, early planning stages, you see—"

"We're listening, Mr. Gross," Chloe reminded him.

"Kent, please. We're all friends here. We all want to see this village thrive and prosper."

"Many folks don't, Kent," Chloe said. "If I've learned anything in my short time here, it's that."

"But look what you've been able to do to update that store," he said. "And now there's a bakery that rivals anything in Zanesville or even over in Columbus." He flipped a hand at Jason. "He's done a bang-up job cleaning up and updating that pizza and sub shop and Barb Wysocki's done an amazing job on that bar and grill. Both now draw the Blue Rock crowd. The opera house is drawing concert crowds for performances and she," he pointed at Hattie, "is putting in a business that will draw the Blue Rock State Park crowd."

"I've already broken some ground and I'm putting in some grape arbors. I'm going to put in a small winery, and a small hotel—"

"Hotel?" Chloe and Hattie questioned in unison.

He sat up straighter in his leather desk chair and waved his hands at them. "Nothing huge. More like a large bed-and-breakfast... an inn, let's say."

"Who would stay there?" Chloe asked. "The Blue Rock crowd is a camping crowd."

"Some of them, yes. Some people just enjoy being able to get back to nature for a day, but they want something a little more refined in the evening."

"What about the church? How does that figure in? There are two other churches in town already."

Jason jumped in. "Wedding chapel."

"Yes," Kent said. "We'd have a place for couples to get married, a place for them to celebrate, a great place to get the cake, a nice place to stay, and places to relax, eat, the opera house as you all insist on calling it, to see a play or a concert, shops to poke around in, and so on for a couple of more days."

Hattie's posture relaxed. "Like a mini resort area?"

"Exactly. A wedding and honeymoon that doesn't cost the moon."

"Why haven't you told anyone this before now?" Chloe asked. "Like the township when you asked to buy the land?"

"I never asked to buy it," he said, "or the church. Jason here owns that. What I have done is I've offered to partner with Jason and his wife."

Jason nodded in confirmation. "Sweat equity from me, mostly, and help to get a liquor license for the winery voted in. Oh, and the church."

Chloe stood, hand on her hip, and glowered at Jason. "So, you've known all along the old church building would eventually be used as a wedding chapel? When were you figuring on telling those of us attempting to restore it?"

Kent came to his rescue. "I made the offer less than a month ago. You were already well into the restoration by then. Look, can we all admit that this is an idea that has legs and could be good for this community?"

Chloe looked at Hattie. "What do you think?"

Hattie shrugged. "Done right, it could bring us all business. I'm an outsider here, though, so I don't know what the community reaction will be."

"You all are," Jason said as he waggled a finger at the three of them. "And, to tell the truth," he said, his tone softening, "the community didn't want me and Kasey to get a liquor license, but they sure wanted that pizza shop kept open. They came around and voted it in." He looked at Chloe. "That store would probably still be empty if you and your husband hadn't come in and bought it. There wouldn't be the bakery either, and you were part of that opera house restoration. This town has its growing pains, but everyone here knows what's good for us."

"So, Kent," Chloe said, her eyes narrowing on him again, "you're willing to fund the restoration of the church in order to use it in your grand plan?"

"Yes, Chloe. Within reason, of course. No grand additions or anything like that."

"Deal."

He held up a hand. "Not so fast! Please do me one small

favor? You can tell Faye Crane the plan because you will anyway, but I ask that the three of you keep it all to yourselves for a few more days? I'm expecting some permits from zoning from the county shortly. I don't want to make any announcements until everything is approved and I can proceed."

Hattie rolled her eyes. "Good luck with the county guys. Slow!"

"It didn't go like we thought it would, did it?" Chloe asked Hattie as they pulled away from Kent's hilltop domain in Chloe's car.

"Not at all."

"That's two suspects we can take off the theft list, too."

Hattie wrinkled her nose. "I suppose. Who does that leave us?"

"Blake, for one," Chloe said firmly. "He may not be doing dirty work for Jason or for Kent, but he always needs money. Mel may have released him, but that's just because she doesn't have a lot to go on. Then there's Molly. We need to get back so Faye can go and talk to her."

"Do you mind dropping me at the house? I need to check in on Aunt Bridget; see how that ankle is doing again."

"Right. Of course." Chloe was silent for a few moments as she thought about Beth and her visions.

Hattie picked up on her change in demeanor right away. "Something wrong?"

Chloe glanced her way. "Can I run something by you?"

"Sure."

"Don't say yes so fast."

"Okay. Maybe?"

"That's better." She let out a breath in a huff. "Have you met Faye's granddaughter, Beth, yet?"

"No. At least I don't think so."

"You'd remember if you had. She's a big fan of yours."

"Teenager then?"

"How'd you know?"

"All of my big fans are teenage girls or older men."

"Yes. She just turned fifteen."

"Older than I thought, then."

"And wise beyond her years."

"It sounds like there's more to it."

"That's what I was getting at. The death of Delores? Beth saw it."

Hattie's head jerked back into the headrest. "She was there?"

"No. She saw it all in a dream... a vision, *before* Delores was found."

"Oh. Wow. That poor girl."

"So you believe it, too?" She turned the car into Bridget's short driveway.

"Absolutely. Lots of people have visions."

"I don't. There are things I can see, like auras, but I've never had visions."

"Neither have I," Hattie admitted, "but I've known several people who know things well before they happen."

"Between you and me, Faye has admitted to having them as a girl, but she says it's been years. Beth's mother, Kris, has never had them. Faye said it seems to skip generations in her family. Anyway, Faye is inclined to let sleeping dogs lie, but I'm telling you that girl is scared."

"Faye won't talk to her about them?"

Chloe shook her head. "She's hoping if they're ignored, they'll fade away as hers did."

"And she's sure hers actually have?"

"That's what she says. She doesn't always want to tell me things, but I've never known her to lie, either."

"Do you want me to talk to Beth?"

"Would you?"

"If I do, it's probably going to upset Faye. She doesn't like me much as it is."

"We can keep it between us. I never said I tell her everything." Chloe gave Hattie a half smile. "I'll introduce you to Beth this week, sometime. She can do her ga-ga thing over you, and then maybe you can pull her off to the side somehow. Someone will just have to run interference with her older brother. He's seventeen and he thinks you're hot."

"Wow, a male not over 60!"

CHAPTER 19–MORE MISSING

The phone was ringing when Chloe walked back into the store. She rushed to get it, since Faye was busy ringing up a customer.

"Chloe, it's Hattie. You and Faye need to come up here as soon as you close. Aunt Bridget just found some more stuff missing. Stuff she's sure was here before."

"We close in an hour. We'll come right over, so sit tight."

"Some of them were pennies," Bridget told them. "None of them graded." She shifted her weight in the overstuffed armchair she was sitting in and glared at her swollen ankle that was propped on a pillow set on top of an ottoman that matched the chair.

Faye shook her head. "Pennies? How much could they have possibly been worth?"

"Lots," Bridget said. "At least, some of them that were from wartime. There were probably several dozen. I had them in little binders designed to hold them for each year. Started those when I was in school. My granddad would give us a nickel every Sunday. I'd go to the store and buy one penny candy with mine and hold my four cents in change until I could get home and see if I had any pennies I was missing."

"Do you know what all you've lost?" Chloe asked.

Bridget nodded. "I know the years I had completed, and the years where something was missing. The pennies aren't all, though. Some of the other stuff that's missing is stuff I had stored with those that I inherited from my grandfather. The same one that gave me the nickels. Those weren't U.S. coins. He brought those coins with him when he immigrated from Croatia just before the Second World War. The coins he brought had a lot of gold content. During the war, they used a lot of zinc."

"Who knows you had that stuff?" Faye asked.

"Most of the family. Granddad willed it to me, and his will was read to the family."

"Hattie?"

Chloe elbowed Faye. "She's in the next room," she reminded her. She could hear Hattie in the dining room making sounds like she was eager to get off her cell phone with whomever her caller was and get back to all of them at the kitchen table.

Her tone was thoughtful as she answered, "Well, Hattie has known about the coins for an hour. Only since I told her they're now missing. She was never around here when she was growing up. You certainly would have met her, had she been. I'd have had her in 4H along with your girls and all the other kids. Would have been good for her. Hollywood! Harrumph! My granddad immigrated with my grandmother and my dad when my dad was four. They didn't originally settle here. Granddad and my dad moved us here back in the oil boom days when the wells were flowing all around here."

"I'm well aware of when your family arrived," Faye reminded her. "No offense meant, of course, about Hatti."

"Oh dear, there was none taken."

"Anyone else around here that you can think of that would

know you had valuable coins here? Blake Wagner, maybe?" Chloe asked.

"I started racking my brain about Blake when Selma brought him up when she told me about her missing coins. I agree with just about everyone in town that he's one to monitor, but that's really from no experience of my own. There have been no deal-ings with the man on my part. Frankly, I avoid him. It's just... just...let's call it a gut feeling I have about him."

"You said some of your latest missing coins besides the pennies you inherited, but not all of them?" Chloe probed again. "Did you go to auctions with Selma?"

"Oh, heavens no. My Joe, he insisted I have some of the stuff from my granddad graded way back in the day. He sent it off somewhere...NGC? NCG? That's what I think they're called. National Coin Graders, I imagine. Once they all came back, I started getting literature from time to time about coins, so I presume I got on a mailing list or two. I bought a few things that caught my eye over the years. Some Morgan dollars and some other stuff. I was just never into it like Selma is."

An old wall phone rang loudly. Bridget rose to answer it. She had the volume turned up so loud, even when she put the receiver to her ear, Faye could tell it was Kasey Myers calling. She mouthed the name to Chloe.

The two women listened in as the pizza shop owner told Bridget she was going to have Jason come by the next day to look at her leaking bathroom sink.

Earlier, back at the store, between the last couple customers of the day, Chloe had sketched the conversation she and Hattie had with Kent and Jason to Faye, as best she could. They had agreed it didn't sound like either man could be considered a suspect. They shot each other looks at this latest development.

Bridget was apologetic when she hung up. "Sorry about that. Where were we?"

"We apologize too. We couldn't help overhearing. So, Jason Myers will be here?"

"Yes, tomorrow sometime, apparently. I dread waiting around for him. He always gets tied up and never comes when he's supposed to, but with my ankle, I guess it's just as well."

"So, he comes often?" Faye asked.

"Once in a while, when Kasey pushes him to come over here."

It was Chloe's turn to ask a nosy question. "And exactly why does she push him?"

"Oh, it's just that with everyone getting older and all, Kasey has been pushing him–and everyone else, really–to bring the family all a little closer."

"He's family?" Both women asked.

Bridget nodded. "Cousin. Third, I guess, maybe. Distant, anyway. My granddad and his great granddad were brothers. His granddad was several years older than mine. He struck out on his own and he settled here in the village when they all came over. From what I've been told, he had a small farm for some time, but he joined the oil boom when it hit, and he pulled my granddad and father in on his oil ventures, too. His granddad is the reason we came to Morelville."

Hattie came back into the room. "What did I miss?"

Faye explained, "Your aunt was just telling us you and Jason are cousins."

"We are?" She shot her aunt a look.

Bridget waggled a hand around. "Distant. Very distant. He would be a 3rd or 4th cousin to you. I never tried to keep track of all of those connections."

"So, you didn't know?" Chloe asked Hattie.

"I'm as surprised as you seem to be. It does sort of explain some of his reaction to me today." She moved closer to Bridget's chair, but remained standing.

"You've seen him today?" Bridget asked, looking up at her.

"Chloe and I went up to see Kent in his office, like I told you we were going to do when I brought you ice...about Sertoma stuff. Jason was there."

"He's not nice to you, dear? Because I won't have that. He doesn't need to be coming around here if he's being rude to you."

"It's nothing. Just a little misplaced envy, I think."

"Maybe I should chat with him when he comes back tomorrow."

"Back?" Chloe asked. "He was here recently, then?"

"He was here to switch my screen door for my storm door off the kitchen for me yesterday while I was out running my errands."

Faye raised an eyebrow. "Alone?"

"I was here to get him started, show him where everything was, but he was done and gone by the time I got home."

"Bridget," Chloe asked, "when did you discover the coins were missing?"

"A couple, maybe three hours ago."

"And when was the last time you saw them?"

Bridget looked at the floor.

"Bridget," Faye prompted her.

The older woman sighed. "You're going to think he took them. It was just yesterday that I had them out, looking through them. I left them on my desk. I meant to put them away, but he showed up sooner than I expected. He didn't mind me running to do my errands. I thought I'd have to wait all day for him. I came home within the hour, after I turned my ankle, and all but hobbled to the door. My hope was he would still be here to help me, but only Hattie was. She got me in on her own."

"Aunt Bridget," Hattie said as she laid a hand on the older

woman's shoulder, "he's the only one that's been here between yesterday and three hours ago besides the two of us."

Bridget reached for Hattie's hand and clasped it. "He may be a little gruff. But he's no thief. I'd bet my last Morgan dollar on that."

"I thought we could rule him out, but now it looks like he's our thief," Faye said to Chloe, once they were safely in Chloe's car, out of earshot of Bridget and Hattie.

"I'm with you. Bridget strikes me as the type to give him the benefit of the doubt, since they're related."

"But a killer? Now, that I don't see," Faye said.

"Maybe Delores really had a heart attack."

"And that Hanford fellow? I've never known Jason to take any interest in picking ginseng."

Chloe rubbed the back of her neck. "Probably unrelated. Something Blake looks good for."

"What doesn't make sense," Faye said, "is why he would take stuff, knowing Bridget would probably realize right away it was him?"

"Desperate people don't always think."

"But why is he desperate?"

Chloe said, "I don't have an answer for that. It looks like we need to talk to Jason a lot more directly and to Molly, too."

"You still think Molly is a part of this?"

"I think they're in cahoots," Chloe said, as she nodded. "Bridget said she got some things mail order. Molly would know that. The post office is very easy access for him being right next to the pizza shop."

"Why would they work together?"

Chloe spread her hands. "Having an affair? They're related

too, somehow? She's in financial trouble like he probably is? Who knows?"

"Stealing mail is still a federal offense, as is opening someone else's mail. I do know that," Faye said. "Would Molly jeopardize her job like that so close to retirement? Why, she has well over twenty years in with the Post Office, she told me not too long ago, nearly thirty years, and she plans to retire when she gets there. She's been right there in that office for over ten of them, maybe longer. I don't rightly recall, but I can think about it. Anyway, what could Jason possibly offer her to get her to compromise herself and put her job on the line?"

"Blackmail, maybe?" Chloe offered.

"Again, over what?"

"Honestly? I'm still inclined to say it's an affair if they are working together. Nothing else makes any sense."

Faye shook her head. "No. I don't buy it. I mean, where and how? We see her come and go every day. He hardly ever leaves the village, and he absolutely dotes on Kasey. For all his other failings, he's good to his wife." She let out a heavy breath and shook her head slowly.

"What are you thinking?" Chloe asked.

"You do realize we should probably tell Melissa."

"Yes. But, I'll tell you what; let's be there when Jason gets to Bridget's tomorrow. All of us. Hattie too. We'll corner him first. Four on one. Maybe he'll do the right thing. We'll save Mel for backup."

"You know, Chloe, I'm still more inclined to think Kent and Jason and maybe even Blake too are all in cahoots and over more than just the church. If I had to finger any of the three of them for the coins and for the death of Delores, it would be Blake, but I think they're all shady."

Chloe asked, "What else could Jason Myers have that Kent might want, besides that church?"

"I don't know."

"You don't think he's made him an offer on the pizza shop, do you?"

"I can't see that, and Kasey wouldn't sign off on that. That's the sum total of their income right now, unless he really is stealing and reselling valuable coins."

" And what's Blake's angle? What could possibly be in it for him?"

"I don't know that for sure either. With him, I'd have to say it's probably about getting money *right now*. He's always right in the moment. If Kent-or anyone-were to offer to pay him to do something, he'd do it."

As they crested a low rise, Chloe slowed the car down to fall in behind an Amish buggy creeping up the next higher hill. "It's going to be a minute before we get to the farm. I hope Jesse wasn't planning on you making him an early supper."

Faye flapped a hand toward her friend. "He can wait, and if he can't, he can help himself. I put a roast and potatoes in the crock-pot before I left for the store. If he's hungry-and that's iffy lately, because his appetite seems to be gone-but if he's hungry, he'll eat."

Changing the subject, knowing Faye was truly worried about her severely doctor adverse husband, she said, "I know we've brought him up, but we've never really dug into it. What are your thoughts about Elias as a number one suspect?"

"Bridget mentioned NGC. Maybe he still worked for them at the time they graded her coins. Delores's coins weren't slabbed though, so where is the connection there?"

"Selma? She could have said something to him about Bridget's stuff. She's a highly unlikely suspect, but if she was just making conversation with him when she passed her stuff along to him..."

"How long has Elias lived in Morelville?"

"Where they live isn't part of the village. They're not really living in Morelville at all, but outside of the village in a township. They've been living out there for years and years, Mildred for even longer than him. Her family moved here from West Virginia somewhere into that house, as I recall it, when I was maybe twelve or thirteen. I only remember her from school. She was little then, in stature and in age. She was a couple of years behind me, at least in school. Maybe three. I think she was only a sophomore when I graduated. She was very quiet back then. Shy even."

"Still seems to be," Chloe said. "You've got to wonder how she and Elias met."

"I've no idea," Faye admitted. "Other than Sertoma, we've never run in the same circles. I don't know them very well."

"Who would know them better?"

"The only one around who has had any dealings with Elias that I'm aware of would be Lucy Sharpe."

The Amish buggy finally reached the top of the rise. Once Chloe could see no traffic was coming, she zipped around it. "Marco is opening tomorrow morning. You're not on the schedule until later in the morning. What do you say we pay her a visit before we go over to hang out with Bridget and Hattie? See if she'll tell us anything."

"It's worth another shot," Faye said as the farm came into sight. She gathered up her purse and steeled herself for an evening of Jesse's aches and pains.

CHAPTER 20–POST PROBLEM

Wednesday Morning, October 12th
Sharpe's Antiques

Lucy tapped a finger on the glass countertop, indicating a small tray of coins in cases stored inside. "Those are the only graded coins I have here right now. The only coins out in the shop, at the moment."

"And I see they're graded. Did Elias Penny do the grading for you?" Faye asked from where she and Chloe stood just across the counter.

Lucy nodded. "Part of that lot I told you about in church."

"Have the rest shown back up?" Chloe asked.

"No. I've got no idea where they are. I think they were taken." Her shoulders shook a little. "I'm not hurting for money, you understand, but the insurance company wants a full police report before they'll pay on a claim. The police want photos. I don't have them, so the police say it's my word only that they ever existed."

Faye said, "Since your niece didn't get to take pictures of them before they were taken?"

"Right."

Chloe broached the subject they were most interested in. "Would Elias be willing to back you up with the police? Surely, he keeps records of what he grades."

"I imagine," Lucy said, "but I doubt he'd help me now that I've accused him of not returning all the coins to me."

"Especially if he stole them himself," Chloe said.

Lucy visibly reacted. "Elias? No. He wouldn't do that. Misplace or forget maybe. Not steal."

"You're sure?" Faye asked. "I mean, I admit, I don't know him that well."

Lucy said, "He can be downright pompous at times, and sometimes he's absentminded, which is why I questioned him about returning all the coins to me, but he's no thief. I've taken valuable things to him before and never had a problem, and believe me, I always made a list of what I took to him because I originally–this is a half-dozen years ago, mind you–felt I had reason to be concerned."

Chloe raised an eyebrow. "Oh? How so?"

She leaned across the counter and whispered, even though no one else was in the shop, "Between us, I heard Elias didn't retire from NGC like he says he did. The word is he had a falling out with someone there and he quit in protest before they fired him." She leaned back and waved a hand in the air. "Water under the bridge now. That may have happened, it may not have. I don't have any way of knowing for sure short of asking him. Until recently–and it may not even have been him-I was always happy with his work."

"She may trust him," Chloe said as she and Faye walked out to Faye's little Ford Ranger pickup, "but there's something about the man that has rubbed me wrong since I met him."

Faye winced from both Chloe's statement and her own effort

as she wrenched open the driver's side door that had a tendency to stick. "Not another aura, I hope?"

Chloe didn't answer her directly. Instead, she said, "I don't see Jason's truck down at Bridget's place yet. Let's swing by the post office and give Molly a poke before we head over there."

"This isn't like her at all," Faye said. "First hanging out, out on the sidewalk and leaving her post while all of that went down with Delores and now not coming to the window, if she's even in here. Wonder what's gotten into her?"

Faye called out again, "Molly!" When the postmaster didn't answer, she said, "Maybe she's back there in the bathroom and didn't hear us come in." She reached around the corner of the service window and tapped the bell Molly kept stashed just out of sight because she hated to put it out. Locals all knew she could hear the lobby door crack open as soon as they turned the handle. The sound of the old brass bell echoed off the cement block walls of the tiny building.

Chloe leaned as far over the counter as she could and craned her neck toward the box section to her left. She didn't expect to see Molly standing right there and, of course, she wasn't. She leaned the other way and tried to look down the narrow hallway that led to the back of the building. "There aren't any lights on in the back," she told Faye. "I think I see something on the floor. Maybe a mail bag. I can't really make it out."

Faye nudged her. "Move over, let me see." When Chloe stepped out of the way, Faye leaned as far right and over the counter as she could without crawling through the opening. "Well, it isn't dark, dark, but the window is covered over. That doesn't help."

"Molly?" Chloe called out from behind Faye, startling her.

Faye's grip slipped and she nearly face planted on the counter. She pushed herself up and shot Chloe a look. "Warn me before you do that again."

Chloe was unapologetic. "Is it weird that she doesn't seem to be here at all?"

"Very." Faye braced her hands on the counter again, but this time she tried to scramble onto it.

"What do you think you're doing?"

"Help me up. I'm going back there."

"Do you think you should?"

"She may be hurt back there. You have a better idea?"

"You're right." She helped Faye get on the counter and then watched as she tried to avoid knocking off Molly's paperwork and pens as she slid to the floor on the other side. She looked to her left. "She's not over by the mailboxes."

"We figured that. Unlock the door and let me in there."

Faye moved to the right, but instead of unlocking the door beside the counter, she went down the hallway toward the rear of the small building.

"What's back there?" Chloe called out.

"I don't think Molly is going to be able to help us...or anyone."

CHAPTER 21—WHAT CAMERAS?

Detective Janet Mason pointed up at the camera that was aimed at the counter area and the customer entry and exit door. "Fake," she whispered, conscious Faye Crane was in the lobby of the little building, speaking with her counterpart, Shane Harding, giving him her official statement. "Or, at least, no longer tied into anything. A deterrent, but no help to us."

Mel shook her head. "Who would know that?"

"I don't know, Sheriff. Anyone who's worked in here, probably."

"Just Molly for years, unless she took a vacation."

"Management then? There has to be someone over her, over this office."

"True. Government organization. I've already been on the phone with the postal inspector out of Columbus who insisted on coming out, even though I told him it's a murder investigation, not a postal thing. He can shed some light on the management chain."

Being careful not to touch anything, they moved toward the back of the building, near the body, now covered over with a sheet from Mel's county SUV, and out the back door.

"Throws our investigation into the missing coins backward," Mason said to her boss as they stepped into the area patrol officers had taped off to preserve the crime scene.

Mel shushed her and waved a hand toward her mother-in-law, Chloe, standing against the tape only a few yards away. "That's between us." She pulled her junior detective around the corner of the building and continued. "I know you've been following up leads that have led you to this office."

Mason nodded.

"It's obvious what we've got here. Someone hit her in the back of the head with that old scale that's laying in a couple of pieces on the floor. This is a homicide investigation and there's no way we're going to keep that quiet. I dare say most of the village knows something already."

"I'll have Harding work on establishing a timeline of who's been in and out of the office today; who may have been the last one to see her alive and maybe see the murderer. She's taken in some packages already, from what I saw. *Someone* dropped those off. People are in and out all the time picking up and dropping off mail too. Someone has seen something or knows something."

"The video sure would have helped."

Mel pointed at the pizza shop a few yards away. "Look what's hanging on their front porch."

"There's a camera, yes, but it looks like it's trained on that porch."

"Maybe so," Mel said. "Can't hurt to ask to see the video, though. Even if it got a car pulling up angling for over here, or someone passing along the sidewalk, it will help us. Whoever it was had to go in and out the front door. That back door is heavy steel and always locked between mail drop off and pick up by someone, usually a guy, who comes around. It's been the same guy for years and years."

"Pays to live here and know this stuff, doesn't it?" Mason asked.

Mel gave her a look. "I'd rather not have any more dead bodies in the village I call home, thank you."

"I'm sorry, Sheriff. That came out all wrong."

Mel clapped her detective on the back. "It's okay. Rough day for all of us."

Kasey and Jason were both behind the front counter inside the pizza shop that was buzzing with customers on a late Wednesday morning at a time an hour before they usually opened. People were crowded at the tables near the row of windows that faced the post office. All the chatter stopped when she walked in, but then the questions started flying.

She waved a hand to quiet the group of folks, some drinking coffee, and others already tucking into bottles of beer. "I have no statement for anyone at this time. I will say this. This is an official police investigation. If you've been in the post office this morning, or observed anyone going in or out of the post office this morning, my detective in the front lobby would like to get your statement." No one moved.

When their chatter resumed, she turned to Kasey and Jason and lowered her tone considerably. "Sorry to barge in, but I could really use your help."

Kasey nodded. "Not sure how much help we can be, but we'll do what we can."

Jason shrugged and looked at his wife as he said, "I haven't paid any mind to anything going on over there in some time. I'm not sure what I can give you in the way of help."

"What time did you both get here this morning?"

Kasey said, "I got here in my own car at 9:00 to get the dough for today started."

"The post office opens at 9:00. Did you see Molly?"

The other woman shook her head. "Her car was already in the back lot when I parked back there. I'm guessing she was inside. I came right in and got started."

"How about you?" Mel asked Jason.

"I got here in my truck about 9:30. There were some siding repairs I needed to do on the back of the building. I can't see the front of this building or that one from where I was, if that's what you're asking."

"Notice anything at the back?"

"Her car, like Kasey said. I was on a ladder, so I was concentrating on what I was doing, more than anything." His tone became sheepish. "I'm a little afraid of heights."

Kasey scoffed. "That's an understatement!"

"I see you have a camera on the front porch. Where's that pointed?"

Kasey tried to answer, but Jason held up a hand to stay her. "Are you wanting to look at the video replays?" he asked.

"If they'll be of help, yes."

"Do you have a warrant? We're not going to just hand stuff over."

"Jason! We said we'd help!" Kasey said, calling him out. "What could letting Mel see the videos hurt?"

"Our customer's privacy, for one thing." He looked Mel in the eye as he said it. "It's the principle of the thing."

"Jason, a woman is dead," Kasey reminded him.

Before he could answer, the cell phone laying in front of him on the counter rang. He glanced at it, picked it up and excused himself, saying, "I have to take this."

Mel watched him walk out the front door and waited to say

anything else while he held it open for two customers coming in.

Kasey waved the newcomers toward the dining room. "Have a seat. I'll be right with you. Coffee or beer?"

"Coffee," said one.

"Beer," said the other. "Bud in a bottle."

"Coming right up. Just give me a minute."

Kasey turned back to Mel. "I don't know what Jason's problem is, suddenly, but don't go away. I think I can still help."

She disappeared into the kitchen. She returned a couple of minutes later with a coffee cup, grabbed a carafe off the burner and a Budweiser out of the cooler as she rounded the counter. She set the Bud down for a second, reached into her apron pocket and slid a flash drive under Mel's hand that rested on the counter. As she picked the bottle of beer back up, she whispered, "You didn't get that from me."

Chloe and Hattie stood behind the tape talking until Chloe thought she heard Jason's voice and shushed Hattie.

"Shh. I can't quite make out what he's saying." She shuffled to her left, along the tape, pulling Hattie along with her.

She didn't dare go too far, so Jason wasn't in sight or in a position to see them, but they could hear him better. He said to someone, "I haven't gotten it yet. It's supposed to come in the mail. Didn't come today."

He was quiet for several seconds and then, in a raised tone, said, "I don't know what you want me to do. I can't make it appear. It will get here when it gets here. There's a whole hulla-baloo going on down here now too, in case you weren't aware."

Chloe and Hattie looked at each other and Hattie mouthed, "Who's he talking to?"

"Kent? Or maybe Blake? Who knows? Wish I did," Chloe said when she was sure Jason had finished his conversation and walked away.

Janet Mason joined them at the tape. "Detective Mason, ladies. Can I ask a few questions?"

Chloe knew Mel's newer detective well and knew an opportunity when she saw it. She pulled Hattie forward. "This is Hattie Novak. She's opening a shop down the street."

Mason eyed her. "You look familiar."

"Long story," Hattie said, "and for another time. I don't think I know anything that can help you, I'm afraid."

"Where's your shop?"

"A few doors down past the pizza shop, here."

"Come up here when all the fuss started, then?"

"Actually, no. My shop is not open for business yet. Another long story. I was down there killing time—Pardon me. Bad choice of words." She pointed at the pizza shop. "I was waiting for my aunt Bridget to call me and tell me Jason, that has the shop here, was there to do some repairs and I was going to head back to the house. I'm staying with her. She called, but only to tell me he wasn't there yet but that she was expecting something in the mail. I came up to check for that. That's when Chloe here stopped me."

"Did you already give Shane...er, Harding a statement, Misses Rossi?"

"Janet, seriously? Call me either Chloe or Mama Rossi."

"Sorry Missus Rossi. Police business. I know you know how that goes."

"Yes. Right away. I didn't see much. Faye went back. I didn't. Not once she told me what she was seeing. I've been married to a cop for forty years. I know the drill."

"Mr. Rossi is retired, ma'am."

Chloe waved a hand dismissively. "Once a cop, always a cop."

Janet looked around at the crowd that was continuing to gather. "Where's Misses Crane?"

"She's still inside," Chloe admitted. *And I hope she's pumping that man for every bit of information he'll give up. Damn it! I should have been the one to go to the back. She won't think of half the things to ask!*

Mel could see her mother standing with her back to the lobby window as she talked with her detective, Shane Harding. She ducked inside the lobby door against a barrage of questions from the crowd gathered on the front sidewalk and shot her senior investigator a look before turning to her mother. "Mom, if you're finished, I need you to step outside, behind the tape. This is a crime scene and one that's already been contaminated by you and Chloe."

The door swung open again.

"Then why is she here?" Faye asked, pointing at Hattie who was following Janet Mason inside. Chloe trailed behind the two of them.

"Sorry to crowd everyone." Mason said. She jerked a thumb at Hattie. "She's here to pick up mail for Bridget Novak. Only medication she's expecting and needs, if it's here and is in the box."

"Do you think it's wise to get into one of the boxes?" Faye asked, looking back and forth between her daughter and Shane Harding.

"I don't see any harm, as long as it's in the box," Mel said. "If it's not in there, but it's here, a postal inspector is on the way. I'm hoping that person will know what to do. The rest of the mail that came in today still has to be put up, and what's been collected still has to go out. I'm betting they have help over here before crime lab techs get here from Columbus, though they're on the way, too."

Faye shuddered. "I wouldn't want to be standing here, handing out mail, not twenty feet from where someone was—" As she trailed off in her thought, she waved a shaky hand toward the back of the building.

"Do you have the key, Ms. Novak?"

"No. Sorry. I was in my shop when Aunt Bridget called me about it."

Mel simply nodded, then went behind the counter moved toward the back side of the post office box section. "What's Bridget's box number?" she asked Hattie.

"Um, box thirteen."

Chloe tried to look around detective Mason at Faye, but Faye had followed her Sheriff daughter through the door and stood just behind Mel where she stared at the boxes herself while Mel found box thirteen. She noted there were nametapes affixed over each box, and she scanned them quickly.

Next to box 13, she saw a box for the Penny's. It was empty, but other boxes in the same column already had mail. *Was he in here already, or did they not get mail?* Boxes numbered thirty and above had little to no mail. She glanced at the mail tray sitting on a low shelf on Mel's left, nestled against the right side of the front counter. It was three-quarters full, presumably with mail for the rest of the boxes Molly hadn't gotten to.

Just above the mail tray, box seven was labeled, 'D. Chapell.' There was an envelope in it, pulled halfway out. Faye scooted closer to Mel to get a better look as Mel pulled the contents of box 13 out from higher in the next column of boxes.

Mel caught her movement and realized she was there. "What are you doing back here? I told you, this is a crime scene!"

Faye pointed at the envelope. "You might want to have a look at that."

Mel glanced at where her mother pointed.

"That's the mailbox for Delores. That envelope that's sticking way out says, 'Littleton.'

"Your point?"

"That's a coin company that sells by mail."

Mel took the contents out of Bridget's box, then looked out across the counter. "Mason, gloves?"

Janet Mason passed a pair of rubber medical gloves across the counter to her boss and accepted the contents of box 13 from her to pass to Hattie.

While she pulled on the gloves, Mel said, "Mom, Mama Rossi, and Ms. Novak, you all need to step out and get behind the tape outside. I know you won't leave the area, so I won't even ask, but a postal inspector and crime lab techs are all on the way, and you can't be here."

Outside the store, just across the alley, Marco Rossi stood, shaking his head as he watched his wife. Nearby, Kent Gross, Elias Penny, and Blake Wagner stood watching, too. Elias remarked, "It's déjà vu all over again."

Kent was the one to call him out. "That's just crass."

CHAPTER 22–JUMPY JASON

Thursday Morning, October 13th

Jason walked through the door to the kitchen and threw his arms up. "This is ridiculous," he said to Kasey in a voice loud enough for everyone in the packed dining room to hear. "There's someone there. He says the mail is there, too."

"What's the problem, then? You can get it as soon as he puts it up."

"That's just it," he said as he grabbed a coffee cup and strode out the swinging door to the front counter, with his wife following behind. "He says he won't put it up; can't put it up."

"Why ever not?"

He overfilled his cup and sloshed hot coffee over his hand as he yanked it away from the machine that let the staff make up to 48 cups at a time. "Damn it!"

"Babe, slow down. Why is this so important that you have to have it, whatever it is, right now, and why can't they give it to you?"

"Guy there says there's an official investigation going on. He's just there to bring mail in and take incoming mail out. He's not authorized to put mail up until they give him the go ahead."

"When will that be?"

"Who knows?" He set the cup down and rubbed his hand. "That's going to sting."

"You didn't answer my other question."

"Sorry?"

"What are you waiting for that's got you so wound up?"

"Just some—" He stopped speaking when a UPS truck slowed outside and stopped in front of the post office. Before the driver could even move to rummage through his truck, a man in a postal clerk's shirt stepped out of the office and went to the door of the vehicle.

"I'm betting it's on that truck. I thought they already delivered over there today. Thought I heard them before." He rounded the counter and headed out the front door just in time to see the clerk step back and the truck pull away from the curb.

Jason waved an arm to get the clerk's attention. "Where'd you send him?"

The man pointed at the store across the alley. "He's got a few things he would have dropped off here. I told him he might rile people up a little less if he asked the names at the store and got directions to the houses." The man shrugged. "It's a small village. They might all be pretty close for him to take right to the door, if he's willing. If not, I told him to bring them back."

Jason was barely listening as he headed toward the village store.

The parcel delivery driver was already inside by the time Jason got there. So were Chloe, Faye, and Hattie.

He interrupted the driver's pleasantries with the three women. "You got something for me? An Express for Jason Meyer?"

The driver looked down at his tablet. "I don't think so, but I don't recall." He used a finger to scroll down the screen. Jason tried to watch.

"Hello to you too, Jason," Faye said.

He just nodded her way.

Hattie mouthed the word 'rude' to Chloe.

"I don't see anything," the driver said.

"Can you check your truck instead of that thing? It's supposed to be here today."

"You're sure it was coming UPS?"

Jason threw up his hands. "I don't know. Probably. They just told me it would be here next day air. That's you guys, ain't it?"

The driver shrank back a little way. "Probably, but around here the post office does last mile delivery for us. I'd have dropped everything I had there today if they would have taken it. Might still do that. I've already spent too much time parked."

Chloe got the younger man's attention. "Is there something we can help you with to get you on your way?"

He turned his attention away from Jason and dipped his head to her. "Thank you, ma'am. Can I give you a few names and see if you can tell me where they are in relation to here?"

Faye volunteered them both with, "We'll be happy to help."

While he read the names from his scanner to Chloe and Faye, Hattie addressed Jason.

Hattie set the bread and jug of orange juice she'd been about to buy down on the counter and tugged Jason aside. "You never showed yesterday to fix the bathroom sink for Aunt Bridget. Do you think you can get to it today?"

He shrugged. "Got a little busy in the shop yesterday with all the goings on next door."

"So, today?"

"I'll have to see what the day brings."

"If you can't do it, I can call a plumber. Just be straight with me."

His voice rose. "I can do it, okay? I'm just not sure when. There's a lot on my plate."

The other three turned to look at him.

Hattie dropped her own voice. "Anything to do with whatever you're waiting for?"

"It would relieve my mind to have that, yes."

"Well then, I hope it comes," Hattie said as she turned away from him, back to the purchases she'd been about to make. Out of the corner of her eye, she saw Jason move back toward the driver. She turned slightly and focused on the corner of the driver's scanning device and said a little chant in her head. *Abracadabra and all that jazz. Make Jason happy and less of a drag.* She blinked twice, then smiled at Chloe who was watching her.

Faye was telling the driver, "Aidan Quinn will be any easy one for you. He's got the big log home on the right about a half mile out on your way back out of the village. Can't miss it."

The driver punched some keys on his device. "Thank you. I think that's all I—" He paused and stared at the scanner for a few seconds then turned the screen toward Jason. "Well now, this is odd. I didn't see this one before. I don't even know if it's on the truck. An overnight for Meyerly, J. Could that be you?"

"Beats me, but it wouldn't surprise me if they messed it up. Does it say on there where it's coming from?"

"No. I'd have to look at the parcel and, to be honest, I don't remember seeing an express on the truck, but I'll go and look around in there."

"That might be my...my paperwork. It sure hope it's on your truck."

The three women watched from the store as the UPS driver emerged from his truck with an envelope to hand over to Jason who stopped pacing the sidewalk long enough to sign for it and take it from him. He had it torn open before the man was back in his vehicle.

Hattie threw a twenty down on the counter as she saw Jason head back toward the pizza shop. "I'll be back in a minute." She hustled out of the store after him.

"Hey, Meyer!"

He whirled around but kept moving, walking backward. "What do you want now?"

"I just want to know why you have to be so rude to everyone all the time. What's up with you?"

"Oh, I'm so sorry. Did I hurt your feelings?"

"Pardon?"

"This ain't Hollywood. Everyone here won't bow down to you."

"No, this place is a lot gentler, with nicer people than in Hollywood...most of the time." She licked her lips. "A place where people keep their promises. What about Aunt Bridget's bathroom sink? Are you coming over to fix that today, since you didn't come yesterday?"

"Seriously? You saw how crazy things were here in the village yesterday."

"Yes, but the fact remains that it leaks."

He glanced at the envelope of paperwork. "Why don't you just call a plumber? I don't see myself getting over there anytime soon. I've got a deed to get filed."

Hattie threw up her hands. "Whatever!" She started to move past him, then stopped. "When you were over working on the door the other day, did you go into the den?"

"Den? No, why? Something broke in there too?"

"You never went in there?"

"Look, I switched out the doors. I was there at the side, and I took the screen door down to the cellar and put it where Bridget asked. Oh, and I was in the kitchen to rinse my hands. Probably a good thing I did it in there because I hear the bathroom sink leaks."

Chloe watched Hattie from the front window. She couldn't see Jason from her viewpoint, but she could tell from Hattie's body language that their conversation was heated. When Hattie moved out of view, she grabbed the younger woman's purchases and change off the counter and called out to Faye, "Hattie just stormed off without her stuff. I'm going after her."

CHAPTER 23–ADMISSIONS

Chloe chased Hattie down. "Hattie, sweetie, you forgot your stuff."

Hattie turned, walking backward, much as Jason had a minute before. "Oh. Thanks. I completely forgot. She stopped and moved back toward Chloe.

"You okay?" Chloe asked the younger woman.

"Jason's a jerk."

"Ain't that the truth? Where you headed?"

She reached for the bread and juice. "I was going to work around the shop, blow off some steam, but I forgot about this stuff. Guess I better get it home."

"How about I run you by the house really quick and then you and I go somewhere where we can chat for a few minutes? I have something I've been meaning to run by you."

At Hattie's skeptical look, Chloe pressed, "Just a few minutes, I promise. I can't leave Faye alone for long. It's almost lunchtime. The 'deli sandwich to go' crowd will descend on us soon."

"I guess we can go down to the shop. I need to feed my cat."

"You keep a cat down there?"

"I have to. She doesn't get along with Aunt Bridget's cat."

Hattie

"I wanted to remind you about talking to Beth."

"Faye's granddaughter, right?"

Chloe nodded.

"I thought this was going to be about Jason."

"We'll get to him in a minute. This is more important."

What could be so important? "Okay." She led Chloe back into her workroom where she immediately went to the open shelves over her worktable and reached for a tin of cat food. As she opened it and scooped it into Freya's bowl, Chloe started things off.

"Beth really needs to talk to someone about her visions. Soon."

I told you before she saw the death of Delores...well, she saw Delores dead and the disarray of her place the night before they found her dead in the disarray of her place. She has a lot more detail than I originally told you."

"That's just awful for her; for Beth." She looked at the maw. It sauntered over and sniffed at the dish of food, then sat down beside it, watching her.

"Yes. It was awful."

When Chloe said nothing else, Hattie probed, "Why are you telling me this? Did she see something that could help the police?"

"Mel's talked to her about it. I was hoping you would talk to her, too."

"Me? About this Delores person specifically?"

Chloe nodded. "Mel talked to her from a police perspective. I hoped you might be willing to talk to her on a little more personal level."

"I mean, I hardly know her. I don't know that she'd listen to anything I have to say."

"You're closer to her age than any of us, for one. Also, like I told you before, she thinks the world of you, and not just because you're a celebrity."

"You know this how?"

"Beth said so. She said you were really nice to her. And, frankly, you can't hide your power from me, and I dare say not from her. Your aura gives you away."

Hattie sucked in a shaky breath. "Excuse me?" Freya moved closer to her.

"I've always been able to tell about most people who have powers. You, you read like a book to me. As far as Beth goes, so does she, but I think she has more power than she knows. It seems to have come out of nowhere, as no one else in the family shows the slightest glimmer of having any, including the child's own mother. Faye said she used to have visions, but she lost them a long time ago. Beth's power must come from her father's side, but I don't know any of them, so I can't say."

"For the record," Chloe went on, "I can see Bridget's aura too, but it's not nearly as strong as yours."

Hattie tried to speak, but the words wouldn't come.

"You poor girl. Don't even try to deny it."

"How? My aura? That's what you see, and you...you know?"

Chloe nodded. "It's my gift. My one and only gift. I can see them faint to strong in other people with gifts, and I can tell by the colors whether they use their gifts for good or for evil, but I can only see them for people I've met and become fairly well acquainted with. I can't walk down the street and point people out as having magic powers if I don't know them."

Wow. Okay. She hesitated for several long seconds and then blurted, "I just want to say, I didn't do the things the tabloids said I did in Hollywood."

"I know, dear. Your aura is bright white with just a touch of gold. Good, strong colors, both."

"What you have...that's amazing. I can't tell about other... other witches, I mean. If I don't know from experience, like with Aunt Bridget, I don't know they're a witch. Sometimes I've had suspicions..."

"Have you had suspicions about anyone recently?"

Hattie shook her head. "How about you? Seen any other auras around?"

It was Chloe's turn to shake her head. "No, just you, Bridget and Beth."

Freya let out a loud meow, startling them both.

"Okay! Okay," Chloe said more to the cat than to Hattie. "There's one man. But, honestly, with him I can't be too sure it isn't just a bad vibe and I'm making it out to be more than it is. The aura is faint, and I really don't know him that well."

"Who?"

"Elias Penny."

Hattie visibly shivered. "Reddish?"

"You can see it, then? I thought you said—"

"It's the only one I've ever seen. I'd forgotten."

"It's the only *red* one I've ever seen, but it's faint to me. Almost pink."

"What do you think that means?"

"I don't know, and I'm afraid to find out." She glanced at the clock Hattie had sitting on her worktable. "Is that time right?"

"11:34? Yes, it should be."

"I better get back to the store."

"What about Jason? Don't you want to know about him?"

"Walk with me and tell me quick."

"Let's just go to the store. I think Faye might want to hear this, too."

"Okay. Mum's the word though on the other thing we talked about."

Hattie made a zipping motion across her lips.

"He claims he never went near the den the day he put the storm door on, then he told me he didn't have time to help with the bathroom sink. He said he needed to go and file a deed."

"Deed to what?" Faye asked as she worked the slicer, slicing Black Forest ham.

"Land, I imagine," Hattie answered. "Did he buy something recently? Did he maybe buy the post office?"

Chloe scrunched up her face. "Why would he do that? How could he do that? You can't buy a post office, can you?"

"I don't know. While I was talking to him, I saw the return address on the express envelope. The USPS in Egan, Minnesota."

"You must have read it wrong," Faye said. "Why on earth would the U.S. Postal Service send something with UPS? They're rivals, for goodness' sake!"

Oops. My bad. Didn't think about that. "I mean, I could be wrong, but I'm pretty sure that's what it said." She tried not to look at Chloe.

"Does the post office own the building?" Chloe asked. "Is it possible they rent the space?"

"Well, now that's a thought," Faye said. "It's a tiny building that was a barbershop for years until about eighteen years ago or so. The guy that ran it died. It sat empty for maybe five years until the post office moved into it."

Hattie asked, "How did you get mail before that? Did they actually deliver it to you?"

"No. Never. Not here in the village. The post office was on the bottom floor of a house right across the street from where it is now. The house burned down. That's why they moved into the building they're in now. As I recall, it happened pretty fast. They were only down and out for maybe a week."

"Maybe they did rent it then, from the owners at the time," Chloe said.

Faye shrugged. "Always was the same owners, the Breyer family, until the post office moved in there. I just assumed the Breyer heirs sold it to the postal service."

Hattie bit her lip, lost in thought. She looked around her. "Do you have an internet connected computer in the office?"

"Yes," Chloe said and sighed. "I hate the darn thing, but you can't place orders with vendors without one, for most of our vendors." She motioned to Hattie, "Quick, come on back and I'll get you set up with it." She pointed out the front window to where one of the lunch regulars had just parked his pickup. "I'll be right back, Faye. Looks like the rush is about to start."

Twenty minutes and a dozen sandwiches later, Faye turned to Chloe. "Aren't you worried she's still back there, alone, in your office?"

"No. I trust her."

Faye rolled her eyes in response, but then whirled away and busied herself wiping down the prep counter when Hattie emerged from the office.

Hattie didn't waste time. "I looked at the county auditor records for Muskingum County. Jason bought the building the post office is in, the land it sits on, and another quarter acre of land behind it nearly two months ago for $70,000 dollars from a Jonathan Breyer of Falls Church, Virginia."

"So that's where he landed!" Faye said. "I haven't seen him in years. Not since his grandpa died. He was in the Army then. Came home for the funeral in his dress uniform."

Hattie went on. "That recording says it's a leased building with one tenant."

"The post office," Faye and Chloe said in unison. Chloe continued with, "He probably had to send that deed somewhere so their rent would start coming to him."

"Eagan, Minnesota is where the post office has administrative offices," Hattie said. "I looked that up too."

Chloe said, "I'd be interested to know when that lease comes up for renewal."

Faye agreed.

Hattie asked, "It's such a small building. What would he want it for?"

"Not the building, the land," Faye said. "The Breyer family owned a lot of land behind both buildings; the post office and the pizza shop. Jason probably wants it all for parking. Him, Kasey, and Molly were always fighting over the couple of spots out front for customers. They could get another half dozen spots or more in back there, and if he razed the post office building, he could extend the pizza shop parking around to that side of their building and park several more cars over there."

"Way to turn the community against you though," Chloe said. "It's nice to have the post office right here in the center of the village. It certainly helps store traffic and bakery traffic for Hannah."

Hattie nodded. "I'm hoping it helps me, too."

Chloe looked at Faye. "What would we do for a post office? It would have to move again."

"The community center, maybe?"

Chloe winced. "That's at the entrance to the village. They might just as well drop it down in the middle of the Blue Rock Forest!"

"Well, we know one thing from this," Faye said. "Jason must

have been talking to Molly about making the deal with the Breyer boy. She'd know who the owner was, I'm sure."

"And he may have killed her to keep her quiet about it," Hattie said.

Chloe added, "And he may have been taking coins to finance the whole thing, because he sure wasn't putting them into the church restoration."

CHAPTER 24–RESOLVED!

Late Friday Afternoon, October 14th
Morelville General Store

Faye's ears perked up. She popped out from behind a shelf she was restocking and called out, "Chloe, turn the radio up!"

"Huh?" She'd been headed to the door to turn the open sign around to the closed side.

"The radio! They just said something about Melissa holding a press conference any minute now about a break in a murder case."

Chloe flipped the sign so hard it almost flipped back. She steadied it, then rushed behind the service counter and cranked the dial on the old radio that barely got reception in the century old building that housed the store.

Faye gave up on stocking and joined her friend and boss at the counter. As a commercial played, the store phone started ringing incessantly.

Chloe waved a hand at it. "Haven't been back to the back to set it to voicemail yet." When it didn't stop, she called out, "Shush!" toward it.

"How'd that work for you?" Faye asked, as she shook her head.

Chloe moved toward the offending instrument and snatched it up. "I'm sorry. We're closed for the day. We're just—" She was quiet for a few seconds listening then she said, "We don't have a TV here in the store, but it's going to be on the radio too." She turned to Faye and said, "It's Hattie. It's being televised too by a Zanesville station."

"Melissa's house is closest and I have a key. Want to run over there and watch? I mean, obviously she's not there."

Chloe shook her head. "No, she's not there, but I'm sure Dana is home. She'll tell Melissa all about us being there. We don't need any more guff from her." She turned back to the phone. "How about I keep you on the line, Hattie? I'll put you on speaker. You watch from there and let us know anything they're maybe showing that we can't see since we're only listening."

"Oh!" Faye said. "It's starting."

Mel Crane's voice cut into a commercial break, saying, "Welcome. I'd like to thank everyone for coming. I'll be as brief as possible and then I'll take a few questions."

"Last night, one of my detectives and a lieutenant brought in Mr. Marc Salyers and Mrs. Rejean Salyers for the murder just over a couple of weeks ago of Mr. Steve Hanford. Mrs. Salyers has confessed, through an attorney, to shooting and killing Mr. Hanford with a handgun she kept for personal protection after an argument over several thousand dollars worth of ginseng she purports he stole. Mrs. Salyers is claiming self-defense. Mr. Salyers has admitted through his own attorney of helping his wife dispose of Mr. Hanford's body, which this department recovered on September 30th. Charges have been filed. The Salyers are being without bond as the investigation is ongoing."

The small group of reporters assembled started calling out

questions. Mel waved them down. "One at a time, please." She pointed at Kate Stull from one of the local radio stations. "Kate?"

Kate asked, "Have you been able to determine from the Salyers' where Steve Hanford was killed?"

"I can't say at this time. Based on the information they provided, we're still investigating several key aspects of the case."

She pointed at one of the roving reporters from the Zanesville television news station that scrambled him and a camera man over to the briefing room at the station house on short notice. "Layton?"

"Any determination on the street value of the ginseng involved in the dispute that led to the alleged shooting?"

Mel nodded. "Mrs. Salyers told us in a sworn affidavit that she suspected Hanford of skimming a hundred dollars or more root off their daily find each day, hiding it in his clothes. We suspect we're talking about $3,000 to $5,000 dollars worth of allegedly stolen ginseng, which they were poaching to begin with."

"A follow-up question, Sheriff?" the television reporter asked. "Is the Hanford murder case in any way related to the murder of the postal clerk in Morelville, which isn't far from where Mr. Handford was found?"

Mel shook her head. "They're not that close at all, and we do not believe the cases are in any way related."

A radio reporter jumped in. "What can you tell us about the postal case, Sheriff?"

"Mel's cringing," Hattie reported.

Faye and Chloe understood why at her next statement. "Poor choice of words, my friend. Her name was Molly. She served that village as a postal clerk for many years."

"My apologies. Any information about Molly's case, Sheriff?"

"Not much we're willing to give away at this point. We have some leads and some evidence. We're looking at all of that. Her killer will see justice served."

The two older women looked at each other. Faye whispered, "What evidence? That envelope? I heard Janet tell Melissa the video camera in there didn't work."

"Then she went over to the pizza shop. Hattie and I saw her. Maybe she got video from them or something from them."

Hattie chimed in with, "Yes. She went over there for a reason, and she was there at least a few minutes."

"I have time for one more question," Mel said.

A man's voice called out, "Is it true that Marc Salyers originally passed a polygraph?"

"You can't trust those things," Mel said. "That's why we keep pressing." With that, she thanked the reporters again and ended the press conference.

"Well," Chloe said, "that solves that, and it frees up Blake from any suspicion there."

"Yeah," Hattie said over the phone, "but it doesn't tell us anything about the coins or about who killed Molly."

"True. We really need to find out what other evidence Mel has."

Faye shook her head hard as she eyed her friend. "Why? Why not just stay out of that? Whoever it is may have also scared Delores to death and may come after one of us next, or Bridget, or Selma. I say that–as much as it pains me that something so awful falls to my daughter–we let Melissa handle it."

∼

Muskingum County Sheriff's Department

"Nice press conference, Sheriff," Shane Harding told his boss.

"You watched that?"

Shane swung a hand toward his computer monitor. "I can't watch *that* anymore. There's only about forty minute's worth of relevant footage. Let me show you what I've got."

He picked up a tablet he'd been taking notes on and read from it. "The only person who was in the post office for more than the twenty to thirty seconds it takes to open a box, get their mail, and leave appeared to be a woman, in brown, low-heeled shoes. That's all the pizza shop camera could pick up, given the angle. Several people were in and out, but their visits were quick. Under a minute. Even her visit was less than two minutes. A minute and forty-seven seconds."

Mel said, "That's not that long to talk your way behind the counter, find something to hit someone with, hit them hard enough to kill them, and then get out without anyone seeing that you were behind the counter where you weren't supposed to be. Anyone could walk in there. Between the glass window in the door that is directly across from the door to the behind the counter area and the big glass front window that looks at the counter and the whole of the box section on the customer side, there's not a lot to guarantee someone up to no good would not be caught." She thought for a few seconds. "No times where more than one person could have been in there?"

"Not that the camera caught, Sheriff. But it wasn't the best angle."

Mel asked, "Anyone appear to be wearing men's work boots and Dickie's pants? I'm thinking about Jason Meyer, for example."

"The pizza shop owner?"

At Mel's confirming nod, he checked his notes. "There were at least three. Maybe more. I could run through again and check." He shrugged. "Most people were in long pants or jeans. It wasn't always easy to tell what shoes they were wearing."

CHAPTER 25-TWO AND TWO

Saturday Morning, October 15th
Morelville General Store

Chloe looked up from the Tastycake display she was restocking and smiled when Hattie came through the front door.

The younger woman looked around. "Just you?"

"Yeah. I try to give Faye most Saturdays off since Jesse is off and wants things done around the farm. Usually, Dana comes in to help me, but she's feeling a little under the weather today. Is there something you need, or did you just want to chat?"

"Chat?" Hattie raised an eyebrow in inquiry.

"That's what I was hoping!" Chloe stood and smoothed her top back over her jeans. "What did you think of that press conference yesterday?" she asked as she picked up the empty delivery carton and pulled the tape to flatten it.

"All I really got out of that is the deaths here aren't related to the ginseng thief's death. What I can guess from it is we can rule out that Blake guy from at least that and maybe from the coin thefts. The sheriff seems to have ruled him out of everything."

"I've spent the last thirty-some years married to a cop. My

oldest son followed in his father's footsteps. I know cops enough to know that Mel's good at what she does," Chloe conceded. "If she could pin anything above petty to him, she would." She laid the flattened box on the counter, rounded the end of the row of glass cases, and leaned over the cash register for support, stretching her back out in the process.

"So, where does that leave us with what we know?" Hattie asked.

"I'm stuck on Jason. He's perpetually broke. Says he can't help with the restoration project because he pours all his money into the pizza shop, yet he bought that property where the post office rents. He needed money to do that, and he needs more money now that he's forked over whatever cash he had for that so he can also work his scheme with Kent. And, he was in your aunt's house the day the coins there disappeared, too. Has to be him."

Hattie nodded. "But, what about Elias? Can we really rule him out? He may be in it too, or there may just be a lot of coincidences."

"And that aura." Chloe closed her eyes for a couple of seconds. "I can picture it. Maybe they're in it together, somehow, some way. It just doesn't seem likely. It's got to be one or the other, but I really think it's Jason. That's my gut feeling." Her words hung in the air as the front door swung open, and Jason's wife walked in, sketching a wave toward her.

Kasey said, "I made chili today and didn't realize I was out of packaged saltines. I'm hoping you have some."

"Not packaged," Chloe said. "I've got the usual boxes with four sleeves."

"That'll do. Guys want crackers with their chili."

"Side wall, about right there," Chloe said as she pointed straight out in front of her.

When Kasey approached with two of the four boxes Chloe

knew she had in stock, she jotted down a quick note to order more. She smiled at Kasey. "You made the right call. It's certainly getting to be chili eating weather. Want me to run a tab?"

"No, no," Kasey said. She pulled a ten out of her apron pocket. "I can raid the register over there. Privileges of ownership."

Chloe chuckled. "I know how that goes. Marco says that every time he raids the ice cream freezer here." She kept her eyes down as she picked out Kasey's change and asked, "Did you hear that press conference yesterday?"

"My yes. It was on the TV in the dining room at the shop. I'm so glad they've solved that. I still have the heebie-jeebies over Molly being killed though, and right next door." Kasey rubbed her arms.

Hattie said, "The sheriff said they have some leads on that."

"Heavens, I hope so." She looked around. "Just between us," she whispered even though there was no one else around. "They didn't have any recordings over there. Mel came to us looking for video."

Chloe played dumb. "Really? Why? What sort of video would you have?"

"Off our front deck seating area. I looked at what I gave her." She shrugged a shoulder. "Not much to see. It basically catches one angle over there of people as they get near the door, from about the waist down. Pants and shoes."

That made Chloe frown. "That's not much."

Kasey shrugged. "Maybe. Maybe not. It's more than she had."

"I'd love to see that video," Hattie said to Chloe after Kasey left.

"Whatever for? You heard her. Pants and shoes."

"I have a thing for shoes. I notice what people are wearing on their feet. Like right now, you're wearing pink Sketchers air cushioned walking shoes."

Chloe looked down at her feet, which were behind the counter, well out of Hattie's view. "You're right. They're so comfortable when you're on your feet all day and you're old like me."

"And very stylish. Plus, they make you almost two inches taller."

The older woman grinned. "There's that too. The higher shelves on the side wall are a bit of a stretch for me. I get tired of dragging the step stool around just for them."

"Kasey must feel much the same being on her feet at the pizza shop all day, every day. She had on Nike Renew shoes. Blue and hot pink ones with a white base."

"You noticed all that?"

"It's my other superpower."

"You know that video is probably a bunch of oil guys in work boots and farmers in muck boots, right?"

"Doesn't matter. I might not know the brand and model of boot, but I can still picture who's wearing what if I've seen them before."

"Maybe you should offer to look at it for Mel?"

"And how do I do that without giving away Kasey's confidence?"

"Hmm. Let me think about that. Unless that is, you can just conjure it to yourself, maybe?"

"Magic doesn't work like that, Chloe. Not mine, anyway."

∿

Later that Afternoon
Bridget's Home

"Thank you both for coming over," Hattie said to Faye and Chloe. She turned to Faye. "I know it's your day off, but I thought you might want to hear this, too. We won't keep you long. Aunt Bridget is in the den. She's a little shaken."

"Oh, no," Chloe said as she shook her head. "What's been taken now?"

"It's not what's been taken. It's what's been returned, but I better let her explain."

Hattie led them to the den where Bridget sat behind a blond wood desk, her hands folded primly over an old-fashioned leather ink blotter that had seen years of use. She rocked back and forth slightly in her seat as she stared at her hand and muttered to herself. A can of furniture polish and a dust rag sat on the desk, forgotten.

Hattie cleared her throat, catching her aunt's attention.

Bridget looked up. Spying Faye and Chloe, she motioned for them to come in, then pointed. "Look beside the door."

The women all looked at a ceramic crock that had a cane and a couple of walking sticks in it.

"The cane," Chloe asked, "or the walking sticks?"

"The walking sticks belonged to Tom. He loved to hike the woods looking for mushrooms and berries in the spring and early summer and roots in the late summer and early fall. Even tried looking for truffles a few times with a dog we had that he trained to root for them like you do with a pig. The dog didn't do so well, but—"

"Aunt Bridget," Hattie prompted.

"Yes, of course. Let me get to the point." She stood and waggled a finger at the crock. "Those sticks are exactly where Tom left them when he passed on. I've moved them around in there to dust, but nothing more. The cane? Now that's a different story. Tom tripped over a root on one of his adventures and hurt his knee. He had to have surgery. The cane was a part of his recovery. He dumped it in there as soon as he could, and he never touched it again."

"A couple of years ago, Elias Penny was going on about his mother at a community picnic Sertoma sponsored. She'd fallen and broken her hip. She was due home from the hospital the next day and would eventually need a walker, and later a cane."

She rounded the desk and walked over to the crock. "I couldn't help him with a walker, but this cane was here. I had no use for it, so I offered it, and he stopped by the house and picked it up after the picnic. He never brought it back, and I honestly never gave it another thought."

"And now here it is," Hattie said.

Bridget sighed. "Yes, here it is."

"When did you first notice it?" Chloe asked.

"Now. Today. I hadn't been looking for it, mind you, so it could have been here sooner...a day ago, a week, maybe. I wouldn't think much longer. It's never more than a couple of weeks between cleanings in here. I abhor dust. I'd have noticed it if it was here the last time I cleaned in here."

Chloe shot Hattie a look and then said to Bridget, "This could change our thinking about some things. To be frank, I was leaning toward Jason as our thief. He may have been an accomplice, willing or unwilling to Elias, the true thief."

"What do you mean?" Bridget asked.

"I'm assuming neither you nor Hattie let Elias in here recently?"

Both women shook their heads.

"Then he had to have come while Jason was here working on that door."

Bridget held up a hand. "Jason would have said something."

"Not if he was in on it, Aunt Bridget," Hattie said.

"Or," Faye jumped in, "Elias showed up while Jason was in your basement, storing your screen door."

Chloe picked it up from there. "He lets himself into the den to drop off the cane, sees the coins, can't believe his good fortune, takes them and sneaks off with Jason none the wiser."

"So, what do we do?" Bridget asked.

Faye was the first to answer. "Call Melissa."

Chloe waved a dismissive hand. "And tell her what? We think Elias was here and we think he took coins, but we don't know? We have nothing concrete to give her. It would be his word against Bridget's if he said he never borrowed that cane or that he brought it back a year ago."

Hattie asked, "So what do we do?"

"I could call him and ask him when he brought it back. Thank him. Offer my condolences, maybe," Bridget suggested.

Chloe shook her head. "That would tip him off that we're onto him. Too dangerous. He's killed for all these coins. We have to think of a better plan."

"We tell Melissa. That's what we do," Faye said firmly.

"We can't go to Mel with this," Chloe said. "Not yet."

Faye still didn't buy it. "Why ever not?"

"And tell her what?" She repeated herself. "Tell her Elias returned a cane, and we think he took some coins? Where's the proof?"

"She could have Bridget's desk fingerprinted."

Bridget sighed. "I'm afraid not. I didn't realize the cane was there until I'd dusted and polished the desk. I did that first."

CHAPTER 26-PLOTTING A TRAP

Chloe said to Faye, as they walked out of Bridget's house, "You know we have to try to catch him, right?" She drew in a breath. "And we have to set it up, so Mel is involved, too."

She realized the last statement didn't allay Faye's fears when Faye said, "I don't think we need to be involved at all. Mel asked us to back off. Jesse gets livid any time he thinks I might be involved in something that's police business—"

"Okay. I hear you."

Faye stopped short of getting into Chloe's passenger seat. "But are you going to back off?"

Chloe climbed in on the driver's side and waited for her friend to get in before answering, "We know things Mel doesn't know and won't believe without some sort of concrete proof. We have to find something for her to work from."

"Like what?" Faye said as she dropped the seat belt link and threw up her hands.

She grasped around in her mind for a minute before divulging, "There's something Hattie might help with...directly."

"Pardon?"

"The video. She can help Mel recognize people in a video Mel has from the day someone killed Molly."

"Do I even want to know how she could help with that? Mel's been here all her life. Hattie has been here all of ten minutes!" Faye scratched her head. "And, for that matter, I thought there was no video."

"There is. From the pizza shop. It's kind of hard to explain, but Hattie is dialed into something you and I pay little attention to."

"We're not going to talk about auras again, are we?"

Chloe shook her head. "No, but that is something that casts more suspicion on Elias for u—For me. He's got an odd one."

"Phfft" was the only sound Faye made the rest of the way back to her farm.

∽

Sunday Evening, October 16ᵗʰ
Hattie's shop

"Who is it?" Hattie called out.

"Chloe. Sorry to bother you. I saw your light."

Hattie opened the back door and let the older woman into the workroom. "You're out and about late for a Sunday."

"I was at the Crane farm helping. We do that a lot of Sundays after church."

"Doing what? Oh, never mind," Hattie said as she waved a hand. "It's really none of my business."

Chloe waved her off. "Nothing that happens out there is a secret. It's a working farm that needs a lot of work. Jesse works a day job because they need insurance. The best time for them to get the big stuff done is on the weekends. Everyone pitches in. Many hands...You know the saying, I'm sure."

"Many hands make light work?"

Chloe nodded. "And speaking of lending a hand, is there anything I can do to help you here?"

"I appreciate the offer, but really, I just came down to check on Freya here before I call it a night." She pointed at the cat, slinking toward them. "Aunt Bridget is at home falling asleep over a ball of knitting. I didn't want to disturb her by pacing around."

"A lot to think about, isn't there?"

"Yes. Yes, there certainly is." She sighed. "Do you think I should talk to the Sheriff? About that video, I mean?"

"I think that's best, yes." Chloe tapped a finger against her chin. "Or, better yet, if you get a chance when she's not busy and Jason isn't around, ask Kasey about it tomorrow. She knows you know about it, so I don't think she'd take issue with that. If you can't tell anything from it, there's no harm done."

"I suppose you're right." She reached out to Freya and scratched her head. The cat arched against her hand for a moment, then slunk away. "What if I see Jason on the video?"

"There is that, but remember, Kasey looked at it. Surely, she would have recognized his pants and boots?"

"Or she's keeping that to herself. I mean, they probably get their mail there."

"True. I guess we need to think seriously about Elias and maybe Jason too and what we know or could easily find out. Maybe even find a way to lure one or the other–thinking Elias here–into incriminating himself to Mel."

"With Mel there?"

"That's the safest way."

"Do you really think he...or Jason is capable of killing?"

"I know Jason far better than Elias, and that's still not saying a lot. I don't think it of Jason...or I didn't think it until all this stuff with the post office. Now I just don't know." She shrugged.

"I've been married to a big city cop for a long time. Over the years, I've learned that people kill in heated moments for very personal reasons."

"I have no idea how to lure Jason into anything, or Elias either."

"Elias is easy," Chloe said. "We ask him to grade coins for us."

"How would that work?"

"Well, first, we have to lay our hands on some valuable coins. Then we try to trip him up in conversation."

"We?" She shot Chloe a look. "First, I don't have any coins. Only Bridget does, and he knows that. If I go to him with coins, he's going to be instantly on guard since he's already taken some from my aunt, at least once."

"That's true. But I've told him, when Faye and I originally chatted him up, that my daughter-in-law had inherited some coins she didn't know what to do with. If I could get some coins from someone like Bridget to present to him, saying my daughter-in-law shipped them here to me—"

Chloe noted Hattie's look. "Don't worry. I'll take full responsibility for them and reimburse Bridget if anything goes wrong." *But Hattie and Bridget should just be able to get the coins back if he somehow outsmarts everyone. They are witches, after all. Couldn't they just do that?*

Hattie said, "I don't know about that. It's really risky for you if you're right about him. And, the other side of it is, what if you're wrong?"

"I'd meet with him in broad daylight, in a public place, like the store or maybe even the bakery. There are always people in there."

"*If* you could get him there. And then, if you do, how do you 'trap' him, so to speak?"

"I haven't figured that part out yet."

Hattie made a face. "Great. This plan sounds better and better."

"It'll be fine. Broad daylight, at the bakery when it's packed, say Tuesday morning. I'll figure out how to get him to admit to something incriminating. In the meantime, you'll have you time to talk to Bridget...unless you want me to do that? We're going to need some pretty valuable stuff to appeal to his sense of greed."

"I'll talk to her. I just have to figure out what to say."

"Just tell her the truth. We're catching a thief!"

"And murderer. Don't forget that part."

Monday Afternoon, October 17th

Beth walked through the door, smiling. She sketched a wave at her grandmother who was behind the register, checking a customer out, then she scanned the store.

Chloe spotted the teenager as she came out of the office and rushed toward her. "I'm so glad you got my message!"

Beth held up her phone. "Is it true, Mama Rossi? There's stuff Althea...I mean Hattie, wants to give to me?"

"Yes. She said an assistant at the studio shipped some things she left in her dressing room, thinking she might want them. Hattie thought you might be interested in a few of the things."

"That's so cool!"

"What's this now?" Faye asked as the customer she'd been tending to left.

Chloe waved a hand in the air. "The studio shipped Hattie some things she left behind. She asked if Beth might be interested in some of them."

"Asked you?"

"She didn't have your number or Beth's. I messaged Beth a

little while ago and asked her to stop here when she got off the school bus. I hope that's all right?" *It better be, because the other plan is in motion.*

Faye's eyes narrowed, but Chloe didn't waver. She stood there smiling as Beth bounced beside her.

"You're sure that's all it's about?" Faye asked.

"What else would it be about, Grandma?"

"No other motives here. I was going to run her over there, but you certainly can, if you like." She pointed at Beth. "You can see she's excited." *Please say no.*

"No, you take her over if she's that keen on it." Faye shook her head. "I have no interest in all of that."

"Grandma, you act like you don't even like Hattie."

Oh Beth, you hit that nail on the head. Chloe smiled at the girl. "Your grandma has just had a busy day. Now let's get you over there." She waved in Faye's direction. "I promise I won't be long."

Faye waved a finger. "Don't you leave her there! You stay with her."

Hattie was ready for them with an assortment of things she'd brought with her from California, and a few things that had to be shipped.

Beth marveled at the pieces from costumes Hattie had worn in episodes of 'The Crestview Crunks.' "Look, Chloe! It's the jacket with the skater girl patch!"

"Try it on," Hattie said.

"Are you serious?" Beth bubbled with excitement. Her hands shook as she picked up the jacket.

Hattie helped her into it. "It fits you well. Do you skate?"

"I've tried. I'm not very good."

"Neither am I."

"But on the show—"

"Sorry to disappoint you, but a stunt double did most of the skating. I did maybe twenty percent. All the easy stuff."

"Could you show me some of those things sometime, maybe?"

"Do you have a board? Because I actually don't. I used my double's board for those scenes."

"I have one. My brother has a better one he doesn't use. Maybe I can borrow his."

Hattie changed the subject. "I have a few more things laid out on the bed in my room. Why don't you go in and check them out? Feel free to try the clothes on if you see something you like."

After Beth practically skipped off in the direction Hattie indicated, Chloe turned to the younger woman. "I really appreciate you doing that. She's so excited."

"I didn't get to bring a lot with me, and I really didn't want most of it, so we probably don't have a lot of time before she comes back."

"Did you talk to your aunt?"

Hattie nodded. "She's not thrilled with the plan, but she agrees that we have to do something."

"We'll take good care of her coins."

"That's not what she's worried about. It's more about safety."

"We're going to be as safe as possible. We may not even get any sort of admission or any useable evidence out of this. We just have to try."

"Let me give you the coins, and the list she made of what they are and their values. Come into her den really quick, while Beth is still occupied."

Five minutes later, Beth screeched with excitement and met the two women as they came out of the den. Chloe used Hattie as a shield while she tucked the packet of coins down in her purse.

"Look, Chloe! The ball cap she wears in that one episode that's in the opening song!"

Hattie laughed. "If you watch that baseball game episode again sometime, you'll see the outfit I'm wearing, a baseball jersey and black shorts, is the same outfit as in the opening credits too. I only ever wore all of that once, but somehow the hat ended up in my personal stuff."

"Really? Wow! I thought you wore the hat a lot."

"Nope. Just the one time."

"Would it be okay for me to keep the jacket and the hat?"

"Sure. If your mother thinks it's okay. You should probably check with her."

"I don't think Kris will have a problem with it, but I'll talk with her with Beth and make sure," Chloe said. "And thank you for doing this."

"Yeah, thank you!"

Hattie smiled at Beth. "You're very welcome."

"Cole is going to be so jealous!"

"Don't you rub it in too hard, now."

"Have to. That's the plan!"

Hattie winced at the girl's use of her famous tag line, but she gave her a wry smile.

"We should get going," Chloe said to Beth. "I'll run you home, then I've got to get back to the store. I promised your grandma."

They all walked outside to Chloe's car. Chloe slipped the packet out of her purse and tucked it under the driver's seat. As she and a still bouncing Beth were pulling away, Hattie looked down the street. She spotted Jason's truck leaving the pizza shop.

Hattie retreated to the front porch and reached for the screen door handle like she was going back inside. When she saw Jason out of the corner of her eye headed out of the village going north, she figured she might have some time to pay Kasey a visit.

"Can I tell you something?" Beth asked Chloe.

Chloe glanced over at the teenager and smiled. "Of course." When she saw the serious look on the girl's face, she changed her tone. "Is something wrong?"

"I had another vision."

"Oh." Chloe bypassed Beth's house and drove further down the road.

"It was bad. At least, I think it was."

"Do you want to tell me about it? It might help."

"There's not a lot to tell you. I...I saw a woman in danger and a lot of light. A lot."

"Could you tell who the woman was?" She glanced Beth's way and saw her shake her head. She pulled in beside Hattie's shop and turned her car off. "So, you don't know? Can you describe anything about her?"

"Pretty young, I think. Older than me, but not old, old. I don't really know."

"When did you have this vision?"

"Today. At school. At lunch, actually. I was eating and then, I don't know, I guess I blanked out. My friends were all giving me crap, saying I was acting like I was high because I was so out of it."

Chloe decided to ignore that statement and focus on the vision. "Tell me about the light. Bright light?"

Beth nodded. "Gold. White. Very bright. Very."

"Was the woman an angel?"

Beth seemed to consider this for a moment. "No. At least, I

don't think so. The light was all around her, and it was over some of her, so it was really hard to see her."

"How do you know she was in danger?"

Beth was quiet for several long seconds before answering. "She was shaking. Not a little bit, like when you cry or something, but shaking really hard. Her shoulders. I could see her shoulders and part of her back and arms. And there was her neck and the back of her head."

"Shaking like someone does when they have convulsions or a seizure?"

The teen shrugged. "I don't know. I don't know what the one word means, and I've never seen anyone have a seizure."

Chloe dropped Beth and her newest cherished possessions off at home, then drove a block up the street in the village and parked beside the store. Before she went in, she found the business card Elias Penny had given her and used her cell phone to call him. Surprised when she got a scratchy old-fashioned answering machine message saying she'd reached the Penny residence, she debated what to do. Finally, she left a brief message.

"Elias, this is Chloe Rossi. My daughter-in-law shipped me some of those coins we talked about before. I was hoping you could meet with me tomorrow and take a look at them. I've got to be near the store all day, so say at the bakery about 10:00 AM?"

His machine beeped, cutting her off before she could leave a return number. *Hopefully, he'll show up.*

As she got out of the car, she looked across the street and down toward Mel's house, next to where she'd dropped Beth off. *No vehicles there. No one home. I'll try calling her at the station.*

∾

"I appreciate you letting me take a quick look at this," Hattie said to Kasey as Kasey pulled up the correct video.

"No problem, sweetie. I just hope you're not wasting your time."

"It would be a bigger waste of time if I went into Zanesville to watch it with the Sheriff and saw nothing. She thought this might be better, but I'll be honest, she warned me that Jason might be upset about it since it's unofficial and all." She hated lying and using the Sheriff to do it, but if she saw anything, she'd let Melissa Crane know.

"Jason's on his way to Zanesville right now. He won't be back for at least a couple of hours." When the recording began playing, Kasey pressed a button on the DVR to fast-forward it. "This is a video of that day. The camera records 24/7, but the stuff you'll be wanting to see is from the time Molly would have opened and on from there, I imagine. I mean, it's hard for me to think she would have let someone into the back before she opened the window, but then it's hard for me to think she let someone into the back at all from the front or the back. That wasn't like her." She watched the time tick for several more seconds, then slowed the playback to normal speed.

"There you go. You're looking in the upper right-hand corner, about here," Kasey said as she traced a line along a small triangle of the monitor connected to the security camera system. "That's a piece of the walk leading up to the post office and the bottom of the door." She handed Hattie a controller. "Point over there. Fast forward with this button. Stop the fast forwarding and play it with this button."

"You're not going to watch this with me?"

"I've looked at it several times. Nothing I saw meant anything to me." She left the office and closed the door behind herself.

Hattie watched the first person come and go. *Work boots.* According to the time ticking off in the bottom corner of the screen, he or she was in and out in less than thirty seconds. While she waited for the next person, she thought about how long it took to collect mail. *If Molly didn't strike up a conversation other than exchanging pleasantries, thirty seconds would be about right for me to get Bridget's mail out of her box and be on my way. It's a small place. Maybe three or four steps to most of the boxes and then back to the exit.*

When the next person still hadn't come along after thinking all of that through, she started fast forwarding; stopping, rewinding, and restarting once someone finally approached the door. *Muck boots. Probably a farmer. Less than ten seconds. Probably dropped something in the mail slot and scooted.* She sighed. *This is harder than I thought, and it's going to be a complete waste of time.*

Over forty minutes into the recording and lots of fast-forwarding later, she watched in fascination as a customer entered the post office and did not come back out for over a minute and a half. She definitely recognized the footwear. *Can't mistake that.*

She fast-forwarded the recording up to the time Chloe and Faye said they found Molly, stopping to see two more customers come and go within thirty seconds.

I think I know who killed her.

She tried to call over her shoulder to thank Kasey as she left the office, but the other woman tried to stop her. "You weren't in there long. See anything you recognized?"

"I'm not sure," Hattie said.

CHAPTER 27-A NEW THEFT

Hattie burst into the store. "Where's Chloe?" she called out to Faye.

"We're closed. And, at that, howdy to you too."

"Sorry, Faye. It's urgent I see her."

"Didn't you just see her a while ago? Her and Beth at your aunt's house?"

"Yes. They left. She said she was going to take Beth home and come back here."

"She did; come back, that is. She was here about ten minutes or so. She shut down the register, cashed out, and then she left again after she talked to someone on the phone. I don't even think she took the time to do a deposit for the day. She said to finish closing up and she'd fill me in shortly. Why?"

"Who did she talk to on the phone?"

Faye shrugged. "How should I know?"

Hattie let out a huff of breath and left the store.

She looked across the street, down toward the Sheriff's house. Neither Melissa Crane's county SUV, nor her pickup truck were in the driveway. *Probably still at the station.*

Chloe was concerned about Beth. The teen's latest vision had her worried that Beth was seeing Hattie in some kind of danger, even though she didn't fully realize it. She called the Sheriff from the store and told her she wanted to see her.

Mel answered her personal cell phone, but she told her mother-in-law she was still at the station. "It's okay," Chloe said. "I'll come to you." *I have something else I need to get you involved in anyway, and I don't want your mom to hear it.*

Before she stepped into her car, Chloe reached under the driver's seat for the packet of coins. She couldn't feel it. She leaned down and reached back, running her hand and arm all around under the seat. Nothing.

Maybe it slid. She stood, opened the back door, and looked at the floorboard. Nothing. She hustled to the passenger side and reached around under the front seat even though she knew the packet couldn't have slid over there. Nothing.

Frantic, she jumped in the driver's seat and drove to her house, where she got down on her driveway on her hands and knees and peered under her seats and felt all around in the interior of her car. Still nothing.

Only two people knew I had coins in here, Bridget and Hattie. Chloe didn't think Beth saw anything. She didn't want to think ill of Hattie.

She thought some more. *Elias! I left a voice mail for him mentioning Shannon's coins.*

Her message hadn't been specific, and she hadn't seen Elias around town, but maybe he happened by and got lucky, she thought. She gave her head a shake. *I'm grasping here...Where are they?*

Try as she might, she couldn't shake off thoughts of Elias and the aura that she always saw surrounding him. Then she thought about Beth's visions. She wondered if maybe Elias had heard her voicemail and had some visions of his own.

Still frantic, she decided to go to his house and confront him.

Before she headed out of the village toward the Penny's home, she called Mel back.

"I'm not coming to the station. Something came up. I have a little problem that I need to see Elias Penny about."

Mel started to say something.

"Can you please meet me at the Penny's?" Not waiting for Mel's answer, she hung up.

The ride from her home on a Morelville side street, out of town to the Penny's home took less than five minutes. She had little time to think about what she was going to say to Elias. Rational thought had left her.

As she drew near to their home that fronted the state route, she saw Mildred Penny backing down the driveway in an older model car. She did her best to school her expression, kept her eyes straight ahead and continued past the Penny's home. She drove all the way to the outskirts of Philo, with Mildred trailing a respectable distance behind her.

She was originally so in a hurry to go to Zanesville to see Mel, she hadn't done a deposit, but she headed toward a branch of the bank they used for the store anyway and turned in when she got there. As she watched in her rearview mirror, she was relieved to see Mildred continue on her northerly path. *Don't know where she's going, but I hope she won't be going right back home soon.*

Chloe drove around the bank and headed back toward the Penny's home. *At least the diversion will give Mel time to get here.*

She knocked at both the front door and at the side door of the house, off the driveway. Elias hadn't been with Mildred, but he didn't appear to be at home either. She tried the handle of the side door. Locked. Back at the front door, she found the screen door unlatched, but the main door locked.

Defeated, Chloe drove back to Morelville and turned down her own street. She tried to call Mel's desk phone once she was parked in her driveway. Nothing. *She must be on the way.* She didn't bother to try Mel's cell number because she knew the Sheriff was conscientious about not answering the phone while she drove.

Chloe pulled out of her driveway and drove to Mel's house, thinking for the short time it took to get there about Hattie. Elias isn't even around. *Hattie. It had to be Hattie. As much as I don't want to believe it, Faye was right.*

Mel pulled in several minutes later. Chloe got out of her car and met her in the driveway.

"There was no one at the Penny's house," Mel said.

"I know. I'm sorry I sent you there."

"I don't know what you're involved in that would lead you there, but I suggest you stay away from there."

Chloe gave her a curious look but admitted, "I think I made a mistake in asking you to meet me there, anyway."

Mel seemed a little taken aback to her. She knew she was by her tone when she asked, "Oh? How is that?"

"I thought Elias took some coins from me."

"What coins?"

"It's a long story and there's no way he could have taken them. It...it had to be Hattie."

"Maybe you better explain after all. Let's go inside and talk before Dana gets home and wants let into the whole mess I'm sure it is too."

When Mel opened the door, a jumping, boisterous Boston terrier greeted her with fervor. "Go potty, Boo. Go!" Mel said, as she shooed Dana's dog out the door.

Boo sniffed at her grandmother, Chloe, then went on her merry way after Chloe gave her a quick scratch behind the ears.

Once they were in the kitchen and Mel started divesting herself of her lunchbox and her gun belt, Chloe launched into her story. "After I didn't find Elias, I came down here to wait for you and while I waited, I got to thinking. The original reason I called and wanted to come and see you wasn't about coins. Not completely, anyway. It was about Beth."

Mel's head swiveled toward the doorway that looked out on her sister's home next door. "Please tell me my niece isn't caught up in whatever mess you and my mother have created."

"No, no. She's not. And, so you know, Faye had nothing to do with any of this, either." She took a deep breath. "Beth had another vision. She told me about it a little while ago. Maybe an hour ago."

"About what?"

They took seats at the kitchen table and Chloe filled Mel in.

"When she finished," Mel said, "Something tells me there's a lot more to this story. How does Beth's vision tie in with these coins you have?"

"I think Hattie took the coins, maybe to go after Elias by herself, or maybe for some other reason. And I think the woman in Beth's vision is Hattie."

"And why would Hattie be going after Elias?"

"Because we think he's the coin thief," Chloe answered sheepishly. "That was one thing I was going to talk with you about when I called you, but after the coins disappeared—"

"So, against my direct order, you're again involving yourself in police business?"

"No...well, yes."

Mel counted to ten, not at all under her breath.

Chloe rushed on. "I wanted him to come to the bakery tomorrow and meet me. I was going to show him the coins. We were going to have you near there too just in case he...he gave something away." *And now I see how stupid that sounds.*

"Are you out of your mind?"

"Apparently, yes. I'm sorry." *So sorry.*

"So these coins, who do they belong to?"

Chloe sighed. "Bridget."

"Ah. She's in on this too?"

"Not willingly, no."

"Smart woman. But, did it occur to you that maybe Hattie really *did* take them back, because she–or Bridget–thought better of the whole ridiculous plan?"

Chloe sat back hard in her chair. Finally, she admitted, "No. I hadn't thought of that."

"Why don't you try calling her?"

Chloe took out her cell phone and called Hattie.

Hattie: "Oh thank goodness it's you! Where are you?"

Chloe: "I uh, I'm with Sheriff Crane at her house."

Hattie: "Stay there. I'm at my shop, pacing a hole in the floor. I'll be right there." She hung up.

Chloe put her phone down and looked at Mel. "She's coming over here."

"This ought to be good," Mel said as she got up and went to the door. She let Boo back in, then stayed at the door, waiting. When Hattie got there a couple of minutes later, she let her right in.

Mel pointed to a chair adjacent to Chloe's. "Have a seat. Start talking and make it quick."

Hattie scrambled into the chair Mel indicated, but then focused on Chloe. "I went and saw Kasey after you and Beth left."

Chloe's eyes got big.

Boo went to Hattie and began sniffing at her feet and legs.

"Boo, down," Mel called out. She shooed the dog away and stood hovering between the other two women. "You saw Kasey about what? Video?"

Hattie nodded. "I know who was in the post office the longest and probably had the time to kill Molly."

"And you could tell who it was, how? That video shows very little."

Chloe chimed in. "The shoes. She notices shoes."

Hattie began speaking again, but Mel held up a hand to silence her. She pointed at Chloe. "We're done, you and I, so you can go on home. I'll tell Dana you stopped by. Right now, I want to talk with Ms. Novak alone. And I'm saying this to both of you. Pass it to my mother. In the future, I'll handle *all the* investigating. All of it!"

As she stood, Chloe avoided Mel's eyes. She asked Hattie, "Did you give Bridget her coins back, at least?"

"Pardon?"

"Her coins. Did you give them back to her?"

"Now, how would I do that?" Boo ran back to Hattie and circled her chair. "The last time I saw them, you were driving away with them."

Chloe's voice shook as she asked, "You didn't take them out of my car?"

"No. They're gone? Oh my, if they're really missing, Aunt Bridget is going to be furious!"

Boo let out a low growl.

Mel pointed at the dog. "Easy, girl. Go lay down."

The little dog crept away backward, but not far.

Chloe advanced back toward Hattie. "I thought maybe you stopped down at the store and...since we didn't want to involve Faye, maybe you—"

"I told you, when you left Aunt Bridget's house, I went to see

Kasey. You took Beth home. When I finished watching the video, I went from there over to the store, but Faye said you'd been there, you'd made a call and you were gone. It sounded to me like you were in a hurry, the way she put it. I didn't see your car anywhere I could see in the village center, so I didn't know what else to do. I couldn't call you then. My phone was at the house."

"So, if she doesn't have the coins, then maybe Elias does," Chloe said to Mel. "What if, to play it all off, he shows up tomorrow, asking to see them? What should we do?"

"*We* should leave the police business to me. That's what *we* should do." Mel shooed her mother-in-law back to the door, waited for her to leave, then addressed Hattie. "You know what, since you don't have the coins either, we're done here too. Elias likely did not take the coins today, and he probably didn't take any of the others. There's no evidence to support that theory."

"But what about Molly? I saw—"

As she had before, Mel raised a hand to stop her. "Anything you saw on the pizza shop video would be circumstantial. We've seen the video too. There *was* physical evidence left in the post office and we're following leads. Leave it to us, please."

Hattie stood. "You don't even want to know who I saw?"

"You saw feet. Circumstantial, if we can even call it that. The crime lab has given us a line on the actual killer. Now," Mel changed the subject, "as for your aunt's latest round of missing coins, I'll have my detectives do what they can to track them down, but understand the murder case is our top priority."

Hattie let out a breath in a huff. "Understood. Now I have to tell Aunt Bridget."

CHAPTER 28-A THIEF REVEALED

Beth sat down on her bed and pulled six coins in their little cardboard and plastic sleeves out of the envelope. She stared at them. As she looked, her most recent vision came back to her, overcoming her. She fell back on her pillows, eyes closed tight, as she saw the trembling body of a woman face off against something she couldn't see again. "Hattie!" she cried out.

She willed her eyes open and began inspecting the coins a little closer. *I knew whatever Chloe put under her seat had something to do with my vision. I could feel it.*

She closed her eyes, this time conjuring the image back up for herself as she weighed the coins in a hand. *Definitely Hattie, but what does it all have to do with these?* She opened her eyes and looked again at the coins. *What are Hattie and Mama Rossi up to?* She got off the bed and willed herself to her window.

Beth looked down the street at the house Delores had lived in. *She had coins. Lots of coins, in my other vision.*

I have to talk to Hattie and warn her. She looked back over her shoulder at her alarm clock. 4:30. *After dinner, when I've seen her go down to her shop. I'll do it then.*

Beth peered through the front door of the shop. She hadn't seen Hattie walk down the street to her store as was usual for her, but she had still hoped to find her there. Only the Mau looked back out at her.

She tried to figure out what to do next as she left the porch of the house turned business and ambled back up the walk. *I don't want to go all the way up the street to Ms. Bridget's house. There must be some reason Hattie gave those coins to Mama Rossi when Bridget wasn't around.* She started shaking. *Maybe I shouldn't have gone up to the store and taken them from the car.*

She considered going to see Chloe Rossi and confessing to what she'd done, but the walk to the Rossi home was even further than the one to Bridget's home. The Rossi's didn't live right on the State Route, and it was getting dark. Resigned, she went home and crept upstairs to her bedroom, avoiding her mother, stepfather, and brother.

After stashing the packet of coins in the drawer of her nightstand, she laid back on her bed and scrolled through her phone, trying to relax.

The dream was horrible. Hattie and Mama Rossi were in trouble over the coins. She woke with a start and stifled her own scream. Visions of Delores passed through her head again.

Those coins are evil! I need to get rid of them now. She pulled on her well-worn boots, the jacket and hat she got from Hattie, then grabbed the coins out of her drawer and stuffed them in a jacket pocket.

Downstairs, the house was quiet. The clock on the stove in the kitchen read 10:32.

She got a flashlight from the junk drawer, put it in her other coat pocket, then snuck out to the garage.

She went into the garage through the side door because she knew raising either of the bay doors would be loud enough to get the neighbor dogs stirred up, including her Aunt Dana's little Boston terrier next door, Boo. *Getting Boo all riled up and maybe Aunt Mel would be bad. Really bad.*

She grabbed a small gardening hand trowel and her bike. She didn't have anywhere to put the trowel, so she just held it against one side of the handlebars and prayed no one would see her as she peddled out of the village to her grandparent's farm, a couple of miles away.

Not wanting to wake her grandparents up or stir up any of the farm dogs, she stopped her bike at the end of Faye and Jesse's long driveway and hiked into the woods across the road. She knew the wooded area well because her grandparents also owned it and she was comfortable there.

Once in the trees, Beth turned the flashlight on and instantly realized she had made a mistake. It was a black light flashlight her stepfather Lance had rigged up for checking up on the ginseng he and Papa Jesse planted and were maintaining to maturity in a way they could hide it from poachers like Blake Wagner. She smacked the light into her palm. *Should have checked it when I grabbed it.*

Beth thought about the city guys who had been poaching ginseng and shuddered. The light flickered and stayed dim. It was getting weak.

She pulled her cell phone out of her jeans pockets. She hadn't charged it. When she saw it on 11% of a full charge, she wanted to cry. Saving it for an emergency, she decided to use the black light instead, for as long as it lasted.

. She picked her way a little deeper into the trees along a sort of path Lance had made. The light picked up little glints of phosphorus paint. *The ginseng!*

Beth went off the scant trail, over to it, being careful not to step on it. Near it, she used the trowel to dig into the ground a few inches, then dropped the envelope into the depression.

I wish I'd have brought a baggie or something to protect every-thing. Standing, she kicked her little pile of dirt back over the hole, tamped it down with a booted foot, then picked up a handful of leaves and sprinkled them over the cleared area.

Satisfied she'd hidden her hasty handiwork, she picked her way back to the trail and hiked a few minutes out of the woods to her bike.

Beth fell into her bed, but she couldn't sleep. She sighed. *School tomorrow. Long day...then after...I don't even know what to do.*

CHAPTER 29-SHOWDOWN!

Tuesday Morning, October 18th
Morelville General Store

Chloe paced behind the counter, fretting. She looked up at the clock overhead again. 9:42. *Where's Dana? What if Elias shows up at the bakery? I need to get over there, just in case. Why did I give Faye a morning off? She'd have been here.*

When her daughter walked in a few moments later, Chloe breathed a sigh of relief, but quickly reverted to worrying when she thought about Mel. "Hey there," she said to Dana. "Thanks for coming down. I just need to give Hannah a hand for a half hour or so."

Dana waved a hand. "Scoot, Mama. I've got this."

"You're sure? Who's looking after Jef?"

"Morgan's looking after him for Hannah today."

"So," Chloe probed, "Where is Mel, then?"

Dana shot her mother a look. "At work. Where else would she be?"

Before Chloe could say anything else, the little bell over the front door jangled. Mildred and Elias Penny walked in. She swallowed hard. *This won't do at all! Not in front of Dana. She'll either expose the lie or she'll tell Mel.*

She made herself smile. "Hey there. Nice to see you two." She noted the odd look Mildred gave her and rushed on. "I was just headed over to the bakery to give Hannah a hand. Dana can help you out."

Elias looked confused too, but she turned and headed down the main aisle of the little general store toward the back and the entry that lead through to the bakery, ignoring him. He called after her. "I'm here to see you. We're on the go today, but you left a message and I wanted to acknowledge that."

Chloe turned. In her head, she resigned herself to dealing with Elias as quickly as possible and sending him on his way. "Oh. That's right. I'd forgotten. I'm so sorry. Come on back here and we can talk in the office really quickly. I do need to get over to the bakery."

"Sure, sure," Elias said. He strode up the aisle with his wife trailing along behind.

The office was tiny. The only chair was behind the desk that held the computer and a digital phone. Filing cabinets filled up most of the rest of the cramped space.

"I have to apologize," Chloe said from where she perched on the corner of the desk. Elias filled the doorway. "I called you about coins Shannon sent here, but I've...well, I've misplaced them."

"Oh no," Elias exclaimed.

"Yes. Thought I put them in one place, but went for them this morning," she lied, "and they weren't there. I was running late. I didn't have time to look for them."

"Goodness, I certainly hope you find them," Elias said.

He seems genuinely concerned. Maybe Mel is right... "I'm sorry to drag you here for nothing."

He waved her off. "Don't worry about it. They'll turn up. Call me when they do." He turned to his wife. "Let's get going, then. We don't need to keep her."

Chloe called after them, "Again, my apologies." *And now I need to get a hold of Hattie, because it looks like we're back to Jason.*

Beth texted Chloe from the school bus as it meandered toward the village.

Beth: Can you give me Hattie's cell number?

Chloe: May I ask why?

Beth: I need to talk to her.

Beth: It's important.

Chloe gave her the number and then texted: Tell her to meet you here at the store, if you reach her. I need to talk to her, too.

Beth: Sorry. She added a frowning face emoji.

Beth: I really need to talk to her alone.

Chloe wondered if Hattie and Beth had talked about Beth's visions yet. She didn't think so. *No time for them to get together. Maybe Beth is seeking her out on her own.*

As she cleaned up and prepare to close, she thought about Elias being there that morning. *Mel. I should tell Mel he showed up here and that I sent him away. That should satisfy her.*

When she called the station, Mel's assistant put her right through.

"What?" Mel said in an annoyed tone. "I'm just on my way out on official business."

"I'm sorry...I seem to be saying that a lot today."

"What can I help you with, Mama Rossi?"

"I just wanted to let you know Elias showed up here today."

"Where?"

"Here at the store. I forgot to cancel him coming."

"And?"

"And nothing. I told him I'd misplaced the coins and sent him on his way. I just wanted to make sure you knew that in case Dana mentioned anything to you tonight."

"What does Dana have to do with it?"

"Your mom was off today. Dana was here to help for a bit, is all. That's when Elias came in."

"How convenient."

Mel sounded to Chloe like she thought it was anything but convenient.

Mel asked, "Anything else?"

"Did you catch the killer?"

The silence on the other end of the line told her Mel wouldn't answer. "Are you still there?"

"Yes, but I need to get going."

"One more thing." She told her daughter-in-law about Beth texting and asking for Hattie. "I think she wants to talk to her about her visions."

"Hattie? Why?"

Oops. Didn't think that through. "Uh, I'm not sure, but if Beth can get a hold of her, she wants to meet up with her today."

"Look, I'll deal with that later. I've got to get going." She hung up.

Hattie's phone rang. *Chloe.* "Yes?" she answered.

Chloe: "Oh good. I hoped I could reach you. I haven't had a chance to call all day. We need to talk about Jason."

Hattie: "Can it wait? I'm on my way out to the Crane farm to meet Beth. She said you gave her my number."

Chloe: "Yes, sure, it can wait. Tell you what; I have to close up here in a few. That'll give you time to talk to her, then we can talk."

Hattie: "What am I talking to her about?"

Chloe: "I don't have a clue. She didn't tell you either?"

Hattie: "No, and she sounded scared. Nervous, maybe."

Maybe I'll close a little early. "Go to her. I'll be there as soon as I can."

Chloe shut off the meat slicer and began the end of day cleaning ritual. *Not doing any more meat or cheese today. If somebody wants it, I'll say this thing is on the fritz.*

Hattie stopped her car up short at the end of the Crane's driveway when she spotted Beth sitting on a fence rail, her bike leaning against a fence post below her.

"Hey there," Hattie began when she got out of her car, "nice jacket."

Beth grimaced as she took it off. She held it out. "You're probably going to want it back."

Hattie shook her head. "Put it back on. It's a little chilly out here. Then, tell me what's going on."

As she slipped back into the jacket, Beth said, "I took something that belongs to you, and I don't mean this jacket and hat."

"You have Aunt Bridget's coins, don't you?"

Beth dipped her head and cast her eyes to the ground. "Yes. Well, I did. I was having terrible visions and dreams, before and after you gave them to Mama Rossi." She stopped herself. "Well, I guessed you gave them to her. I saw her put them under her car seat and I kind of got a weird feeling about whatever she had because I'd already had a vision I was going to tell her about."

"We should talk about your visions, you and I, but first, I need to know what happened to those coins."

"I...I hid them. Buried them. In the woods, over there." She pointed across the road.

"Show me," Hattie said.

Beth jumped off the fence rail and led the way across the old township road, toward the path into the woods. "I did it last night when it was dark, so I didn't go in very far." She picked her way forward along the narrow path for a few minutes, watching for a disturbance in the leaves where she'd gone off the trail. She knew Lance and her grandpa planted the ginseng on a slight hillside under the shade of some larger sugar maple trees.

When she spotted what looked like the right area, she veered off the path to her right.

Hattie put out a hand, stopping her, and whispered, "Did you hear that?"

Beth cocked an ear and listened for several seconds before whispering back, "The birds?"

"No." She listened again for several seconds, then conceded, "I don't hear it now. Never mind, I guess." *No sense scaring her more than she already is.*

Beth stopped short of two maples and surveyed the ground. "Some of this is ginseng with the leaves clipped off," she explained to Hattie. "My papa and my step-dad are trying to let it grow for a couple more years without poachers finding it."

"Oh." Hattie scanned the ground too, but she wasn't sure what she was supposed to be avoiding. "How about I just stay put right here?"

Beth nodded and pointed. "I buried them just to the side of the second tree there, I think." She took the spade from her pocket that she'd returned to the garage the previous night only to retrieve it again after school. After scooping away leaves around the base of the tree, she found a spot with both loose and packed dirt and dug with a light, easy touch.

The hair on the back of Hattie's neck stood up. She half

turned and looked back toward the path they took into the woods. She shuddered when she saw Elias Penny picking his way slowly toward them.

"Beth!" Hattie hissed at the girl.

The teenager looked her way, then stood. She held the trowel behind her leg to hide it.

"Digging for truffles?" Elias inquired. He gave off a laugh. "Even if you could find many of them in Ohio, you're looking under the wrong kind of tree. That's a sugar maple."

"I know," Beth said.

He ignored her and continued with a mini lesson as he drew closer to them, but he stayed on the trail. "Truffles grow under oaks, or pine most often around here; when you can find them at all, that is. Ohio weather isn't the best for them."

Hattie jumped in before he could go on. "What brings you out here, Elias? Doing some truffle hunting yourself?" *Fat chance.* She flexed her fingers, hoping if things got crazy with him, she could conjure enough magic to slow him down and let Beth get away.

"No. No. That wouldn't be right of me. This is private property, is it not?" He looked at Beth for an answer.

"Yes. My grandparents land."

"I'm just out walking," he answered. "Something called me here."

Hattie raised an eyebrow. "Called you?"

"I've not been out here before, but I used to walk a few miles every day. My dear mother liked a little park that was near her home. I would take her there when she felt up to it. There's a groomed trail near my house I take sometimes. This is rougher. I'm not sure what drew me here."

Hattie noted his aura. *Very light pink, almost white.* The feeling of threat lifted, and she relaxed her hands.

She looked at Beth. She'd never seen an aura surrounding

the teenager, like Chloe said she could see, but Hattie could feel something special about her since she'd gotten to know her. Hattie sensed the girl had some sort of power; power she was wholly unaware of. She thought Beth looked scared. She flexed her hands again, but she willed them to stay at her sides, and she trained her eyes on Elias.

"Do you think it would be okay if I continue along?" Elias asked Beth.

In a shaky voice, the girl replied, "The trail really isn't very good."

"I'll be careful."

Beth looked at Hattie, a plea plain in her eyes.

"Maybe it would be best if you check with Mr. Crane first," Hattie suggested. "We'll be heading back into town in a minute, and you'll be on your own. He'll want to know you're out here."

Elias dipped his head in a nod. "You're right, of course, and frankly I probably should just go."

Elias turned about then, but before he took a step, a woman's voice rang out from a thicket beyond where Beth was standing near the sugar maples. "Not so fast! The whole lot of you stay put!"

"Mildred?" Elias called out.

"That's right. It's me," she said as she rounded the thicket and headed straight for Beth.

Hattie looked at Mildred Penny's feet and swallowed hard. *Mary Janes from the video. I was right.* "Run Beth!"

Mildred swung a hand in the girl's direction, stopping her.

Beth tried to move, but she couldn't.

"What's your hurry, pet?" Mildred asked. She held up the other hand to Hattie and Elias. "Don't move, or you'll get the same."

She approached Beth and grabbed at the trowel. As she waved it before the teen's eyes, she commanded her, "Get down there and finish digging. I know what's down there, and I want it."

Beth dropped to her knees and did as she was told.

As Hattie's mind whirred, Elias tried to question his wife. "Mildred, what's this all about?"

"I'm leaving you, Elias. I've had it. Despite our powers, I'm tired that we're always broke. We've lived in hiding as mortals for far too long."

"That was to protect you!"

"I hardly need protection now. Those protests are far in the past...forgotten. There's little I can do to save mother earth now." She glanced over at Beth who was digging with a gentle touch. "I've been taking coins I know are quite valuable after years of listening to you prattle on as you graded and slabbed them for other people. Gathering myself a nice little nest egg. That's the plan." She looked at Hattie let out a loud cackle, but then cut it short. "At least, it was."

"So much so you killed for it?" Hattie asked.

"No." Elias said. "No. She didn't."

"I did," Mildred said. "Well, Molly, anyway. She caught me trying to sneak a packet of coins and made a scene. You'd have thought they were hers, not just mail! As for Delores, I didn't even know she was there. I'm afraid we both gave each other a scare."

"But she died," Hattie said.

Mildred tossed her head. "She'd have likely had a heart attack that night, anyway. She was ancient."

Elias was taken aback. "Mildred!"

She waved her husband off. "Enough from you! More than enough with countless years of your self-important puffery!"

Beth stood and held out the dirt-stained envelope with a shaking hand.

Mildred snatched it from her.

"Am I to assume those are Mrs. Rossi's missing coins?" Elias asked.

Hattie cleared her throat. "They're actually Aunt Bridget's." She looked at Mildred. "You've got what you wanted. Now go."

"And leave all of you behind to tattle? I think not."

Now Elias spoke with fear in his voice. "You can't kill us all. You won't be able to get away with that. You'll be found and jailed. Your powers can't defeat metal bars!"

That was all Hattie needed to hear. *I'm not powerful, but I have help and youth and she's a witch out of practice.*

"Beth, do what I do, and repeat after me."

"What?"

"Do it!" Hattie held her hands out toward Mildred and chanted "Winds of the trees, I call on thee to bind thou to thee." She nodded to Beth who was now holding her hands out, the trowel still in her right hand, and began again with Beth also chanting along. "Winds of the trees, I call on thee to bind thou to thee."

Mildred stumbled backward toward one of the sugar maples and appeared to be paralyzed there.

With her hands still raised, Hattie called out to Beth, "Call 911! Run to the farm. Get help here."

Beth flung the trowel, dug in her pocket for her phone, and began running to the path, brushing by Elias Penny as she went.

She didn't get far as the cavalry arrived in the form of Mel and one of her deputies, with Chloe Rossi and Faye Crane trailing directly behind.

"Everybody freeze!" Mel called out.

Hattie lowered her hands, but otherwise stayed in place.

Faye ignored her daughter's instructions and rushed to Beth. "Are you okay?"

"Fine, grandma."

"Aunt Mel," Beth said as she pointed at Mildred, "That woman stole coins and killed the post office lady, and she doesn't even act sorry for any of it."

EPILOGUE

Sunday, October 23rd
The Crane Family Farm
Morelville, Ohio

"I've returned all the coins to their rightful owners or heirs," Mel told the family assembled on the front porch after dinner.

Faye smiled, and Chloe clapped her hands together. "That's wonderful for Bridget and Selma," Chloe said.

"Yes, and Bridget mentioned when I delivered hers that she'll be auctioning off the ones she originally intended to auction and donating the proceeds to the restoration of the church… whatever Kent doesn't cover, as she put it. She wanted me to be sure and tell you."

Faye nodded. "That's wonderful too. But I can't get too excited, I'm afraid. Two people needlessly lost their lives in Mildred's pursuit of all of those coins."

Mel stood as she said, "I know, Mom. That's the tough thing

here. And on top of that, Mildred's lawyer is trying to get Delores' death thrown out." She leaned against a stone post facing the usual Sunday mix of Cranes and Rossis. "They charged her for negligent homicide there, but I don't think anything but the theft will stick."

Mel's father asked, "You were on your way out here anyway Tuesday when you nabbed the Penny woman. What for?"

"I suppose it's no secret now. Early on, we got a crime lab report matching the prints we found at Delores Chappel's place to Mildred Penny. She was one of the people we had eyes on, but we couldn't prove anything since there were so many sets of prints down there."

"I don't understand," Chloe said. "Why would you have had a match on Mildred of all people? The woman is a mouse, or at least she seemed like one."

Mel nodded, rocking her whole body forward from the post. "I always thought of her as quiet and pretty subservient to Elias too, but it turns out she has a history." She was interrupted by the sound of gravel crunching in the driveway. They all turned to look as Hattie's car approached the front of the house.

Beth rushed off the porch, calling over her shoulder, "She came! I can't believe it!"

They all watched as Hattie stopped her car and got out. "I hope I'm not interrupting. Beth messaged me and asked me to come out."

"It's fine," Chloe called out before Faye could say anything. "Come on up. Mel was just giving us the lowdown on Mildred."

Mel waited until Hattie reached the porch, then continued. "I was saying Mildred seemed to be one thing, but back in the day she was quite another. She has an arrest record for–we'll call it mischief making–and violent protests in the early '80s around new coal power plants and later nuclear power plants along the Ohio River at the Ohio and West Virginia state line. Weird things happening at the plants and such that the investigators at the time could never quite prove she was involved in."

Faye said, "I never heard any of that. She would have had to have been young then. Right out of high school or in college, maybe."

"Anyway," Mel went on, "When her prints turned up on the edge of a desk at the back of the post office too, we started looking for her. She's a wily one, though. Harder to track down than you would think."

Chloe shot a glance at Hattie. Hattie looked down at her feet.

"One of my deputies thought he spotted her heading out this way. I was on my way back to the village anyway, so I figured I'd come and check things out."

"Good thing you did," Faye said. "Why who knows what the woman would have done? She had poor Beth scared half to death."

"I was fine, Grandma. Hattie was there."

Hattie gave the girl a small smile. "Your grandmother was just worried about you."

Faye pointed a finger at Chloe, then at Hattie. "It was the little scheme the two of you cooked up that got her into that mess. We're all lucky Mel came along when she did."

"Yes," Hattie said. "We certainly are."

BETH RAN a brush down her horse's neck. "Thanks for coming out here," she said to Hattie. "I know Grandma blames you for what happened the other day."

Hattie leaned over the stall gate and gave the horse's nose a pat. "I wanted to talk to you, anyway. That's why I was originally thought I was coming out here Tuesday. I thought you wanted to talk about some things."

"Like that thing you had me do in the woods to stop that woman?"

"Well, that too, but not for starters." She drew in a breath. "Tell me about your visions."

Beth shot her a look. "There's not much to tell. I get them sometimes, but not all the time. When I get them, they're kind of..." She trailed off.

"Scary?"

The teenager nodded. "Usually."

"I know you don't think this now, Beth, but your visions? They're a gift. And also, you use them right. When you have them, you tell people who can help you with what you see. That's important. That and having people who believe you."

"Mama Rossi believes me. I don't think Grandma does."

"She does, Beth. Trust me. She's just scared for you. And, you know what? I believe you too. You can always tell me when you see things."

"Always?"

"Yes. Always."

"Why?"

Such a simple question and so hard at the same time. "Well, --"

"Do you have them, too?"

"No." Hattie shook her head. "I never have. I have other... gifts, and so do you."

"Like the magic?"

"Yes. I have the gift of magic. I'm a witch. You have the gift too and, it would seem, with great power."

"I don't feel like I have magic. I don't know anyone who does, besides you, anyway. Does my mom have it?"

Hattie shook her head no. "I don't think so."

"Then how would I have gotten it?"

"How much do you know about your father and his family?"

"Not much," the girl admitted. "Mom never married him and she won't let me near them."

Telling. "What about your brother?"

"He has a different dad."

"Ah."

"What can I do with it?"

"With magic? Lots of stuff, or nothing. That's up to you."

"I don't know anything about it."

"Yet. You don't know anything yet."

"Will you teach me?"

Hattie grinned. "Of course. As much as I can, anyway. I think you'll be a lot more powerful than me when it's all said and done."

"I don't think my Grandma would approve. We should probably keep it quiet."

"That's the plan."

AFTERWORD

This story is entirely fictional, but I wanted to clarify something. Sertoma is an actual organization in the United States and Canada. Sertoma is an acronym for 'Service to Mankind.' Sertoma service clubs exist in big cities and in small villages across both countries.

In the U.S., the national organization focuses on hearing related causes and needs. Individual clubs get involved in a lot more localized programs and in community outreach.

There's a Sertoma service club in the tiny little village I live in, population under 500. Year round, club members raise funds through various means and put a lot of the money they raise right back into the community. I'm not a member, but I'm a contributor, and I and members of my family have been recipients of their generosity multiple times.

If you're in the U.S. or in Canada and you're looking for a service organization to join or to give to, consider your local Sertoma club.

~Anne

PLEASE LEAVE A REVIEW

If you've enjoyed this book, please tell your friends about it. Did you know you can lend the book? To do so, simply follow the instructions Amazon provides for loaning a book. Meanwhile, if you have a chance, I would really appreciate an honest review on Amazon. You can review this book by following this link: The Conjuring Comedienne. Thank you!

ABOUT THE AUTHOR

Anne Hagan is the author of over twenty works of fiction in the mystery, romance, and thriller genres. She writes of family, friends, love, murder, and mayhem in no particular order and often all in the same story. She's a half owner of the weekly discount eBook newsletter, MyLesfic, a wife, parent, foster parent, and an Army veteran. She draws from all of those experiences when she writes because truth is often stranger than fiction.

CHECK ANNE OUT ON THE WEB, ON FACEBOOK OR ON TWITTER:

For the latest information about upcoming releases, other projects, sample chapters and everything personal, check out Anne's **site** at https://AnneHaganAuthor.com/ or like Anne on **Facebook** at https://www.facebook.com/AuthorAnneHagan. You can also connect with Anne on **Twitter** @AuthorAnneHagan.

JOIN ANNE'S EMAIL LIST

Are you interested in **free books**? How about **free short stories**? For those and all the latest news on new releases, **opportunities to get review copies of all of her new releases** and more, please consider joining Anne's email list at: https://www.AnneHagan-Author.com by filling in the pop up or using the brief form in the sidebar.

ALSO WRITTEN BY THE AUTHOR

A spinoff of Anne's Morelville Mysteries series, The Morelville Cozies series feature meddling mother sleuths Faye Crane and Chloe Rossi getting mixed up in mysteries all their own.

The Passed Prop: The Morelville Cozies–Book 1

Chloe Rossi wants to retire with her husband and move away from suburban sprawl to bucolic Morelville; the only trouble is, Morelville is experiencing its worst crime wave ever, and Marco Rossi wants no part of a move there. What to do?

Opera House Ops: The Morelville Cozies–Book 2

Murder and other sinister goings-on at a vacant 1800s era opera house in Morelville and a modern-day property developer who wants to raze the historic building for his own gain have the village residents all tied up in knots and Faye Crane trying to play savior to history.

The books of the Morelville Mysteries series Anne's Sapphic/Women Loving Women themed mystery/romance series that spawned the Morelville Cozies (see book 5):

Relic: The Morelville Mysteries–Book 1–The first Dana and Sheriff Mel mystery and the first book in the Morelville saga. Please click the link above, which will take you to Anne's site, where you can get links to get this book.

Cases collide for two star crossed ladies of law enforcement!

Busy Bees: The Morelville Mysteries–Book 2

Romance and Murder Mix in the Latest Story Featuring Sheriff Mel Crane and Special Agent Dana Rossi!

Dana's Dilemma: The Morelville Mysteries–Book 3–The relationship matures between Mel and Dana in an installment that features a breaking Amish character, an ex-girlfriend, a conniving politician, and murder.

Elections and Old Loves Combine with Deadly Results in a Romantic Mystery Featuring Sheriff Mel Crane and Special Agent Dana Rossi!

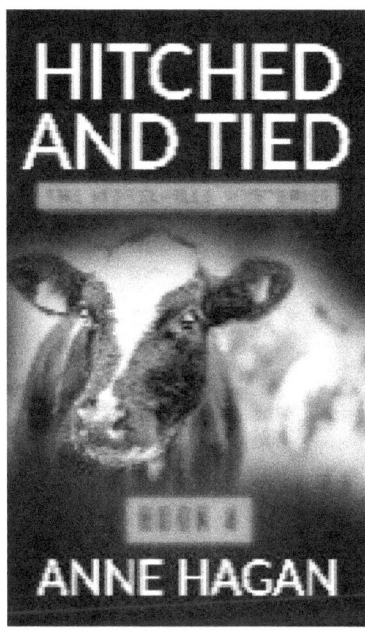

Hitched and Tied: The Morelville Mysteries–Book 4

Mel and Dana attempt to bring their growing romantic relationship full circle, but family, duty, and family duties all conspire to get in the way.

Viva Mama Rossi!: The Morelville Mysteries–Book 5–The 5th tale in the Morelville Mysteries and the book that gives fans a full introduction to future Morelville Cozies series sleuths Faye Crane (Mel's mom) and Chloe Rossi (Dana's Mama). The two series stand-alone, but they're certainly better together.

A delayed honeymoon getaway takes a deadly turn for newly-weds Mel and Dana; meanwhile, two meddling mothers won't let sleeping fisherman lie in the latest Morelville Mystery.

A Crane Christmas: The Morelville Mysteries–Book 6

Is it the Christmas season or the 'silly season'?

Mad for Mel: The Morelville Mysteries–Book 7

Rival gangs will stop at nothing to gain sole control of the drug trade in Muskingum County, and they've picked Valentine's week to create a firestorm of murder and mayhem as they battle each other for supremacy.

Hannah's Hope: The Morelville Mysteries–Book 8

A young mother with a troubled past seeks help from Mel and Dana, but is their effort to assist her too little, too late?

The Turkey Tussle: The Morelville Mysteries–Book 9

The old-fashioned country village of Morelville holds a secret.

Sullied Sally: The Morelville Mysteries–Book 10

An unsolved murder, over 40 years in the past, leads to the discovery of a new victim and the return of an old stalker.

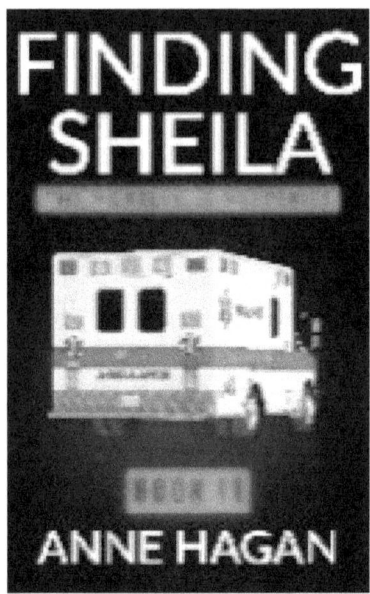

Finding Sheila: The Morelville Mysteries–Book II

A woman, imprisoned for manslaughter, disappears without a trace during transport between states, and it's all up to Dana to find her.

Tennessee Bound: The Morelville Mysteries–Book 12

The politics and the paper-pushing are wearing on Sheriff Mel. Will she chuck it all?

Three multi-eBook boxed sets of the Morelville Mysteries works by Anne Hagan are also available for purchase.

The Morelville Mysteries Full Circle Collection is a five eBook set that contains the first four Morelville Mysteries novels and an exclusive <u>Companion Guide</u> that is only available with this set.

The Morelville Mysteries: Books 5-8 Collection

The Morelville Mysteries: Books 9-12 Collection

~

Steel City Confidential–Anne's first legal thriller (AKA The Thelma and Louise Book)

Clients hide things from their lawyers all the time. Pam Wilson makes it an art form.